Patricia Clapp

THE
TAMARACK
TREE

A Novel of the Siege of Vicksburg

Puffin Books

PUFFIN BOOKS
Published by the Penguin Group
Viking Penguin Inc., 40 West 23rd Street, New York, New York 10010, U.S.A.
Penguin Books Ltd, 27 Wrights Lane, London W8 5TZ, England
Penguin Books Australia Ltd, Ringwood, Victoria, Australia
Penguin Books Canada Ltd, 2801 John Street, Markham, Ontario, Canada L3R 1B4
Penguin Books (N.Z.) Ltd, 182–190 Wairau Road, Auckland 10, New Zealand

Penguin Books Ltd, Registered Offices: Harmondsworth, Middlesex, England

First published in the United States of America by Lothrop, Lee & Shepard Books,
a division of William Morrow and Company, Inc., 1986
Published in Puffin Books 1988
by arrangement with William Morrow and Company, Inc.

Library of Congress Cataloging in Publication Data
Clapp, Patricia.   The tamarack tree/by Patricia Clapp.
p.   cm.
Summary: An eighteen-year-old English girl finds her loyalties divided and all her
resources tested as she and her friends experience the terrible physical and emotional
hardships of the forty-seven-day siege of Vicksburg in the spring of 1863.
ISBN 0-14-032406-2
1. Vicksburg (Miss.)—History—Siege, 1863—Juvenile fiction.   2. United States—
History—Civil War, 1861–1865—Juvenile fiction.   [1. Vicksburg (Miss.)—History—
Siege, 1863—Fiction.   2. United States—History—Civil War, 1861–1865—Fiction.]
I. Title. [Fic]—dc 19   88-1133

Printed in the United States of America by Arcata Graphics, Kingsport, Tennessee
Set in DeVinne

FOR EDWARD

and for his great-grandson James Edward,
the first of the next generation.

THE
TAMARACK
TREE

The Beginning

I WAS THIRTEEN WHEN MAMMA DIED, FOURTEEN WHEN Derek and I arrived in the States. I am seventeen now and it's anybody's guess whether or not I live to be eighteen.

It gets a little worse each day. Today it is like a rending thunderstorm, cracking and crashing almost over my head. I have been pacing from one end of the house to the other, wishing Derry would come home, but knowing that the afternoon is but half over, and it is far too early to expect him. My walking back and forth takes me to the door of the kitchen, and I look in at Amanda and her little daughter, Betsy. Amanda, that usually calm, beautiful black woman, has stuffed her ears with cotton and sits in the rocking chair, pushing her feet violently against the board floor. Betsy huddles in her mother's arms, her eyes squeezed shut, small hands covering her ears against the noise. I can remember my own mother's arms making me feel safe and protected, too.

This is ridiculous! Marching from room to room, from wall to wall, from door to window will accomplish nothing. It simply makes me more agitated. Derry would say, "Find a scrap of paper and write something! Anything! You are always more content with a pen and paper in front of you." But what will I write? And there is so little paper.... He would say, "Write the date! Write your name. Write *my* name. It doesn't matter. Just start writing!" Very well, dear brother, I will try. Paper is hard to come by—everything is hard to come by!—but there are a few rolls of wallpaper in a cupboard and I can use the backs of those. So I sit myself down, my dress billowing out over my wilted petticoats—I no longer bother with my hoop—and gaze at the sheet of paper.

"Write the date!" I'm not sure I know the date. The year is 1863, I am certain of that, it being the most terrifying year I have ever experienced, and the month is April—I shall be eighteen in a week or so—but as to the actual date ... but then, what does it matter? Each day is much like the one before, except that each is more frightening. I tell myself that everything ends eventually, and then wonder whether I shall be around to see the end of this. Enough! It is not making me any calmer.

My name. My name is Rosemary Monica Stafford Leigh. The English often give their children a great variety of names. My brother is Derek Charles Gregory Leigh. He is eight years older than I, so he must be— good heavens! Derry is twenty-six! And Mamma, had she lived, would be—but what's the use of that? Mamma, dear Mamma, died four years ago. It took her a long time to die, and I was with her all the while. There was time for Derry to reach London and be with us for close to a month before the end finally came. Father had died a year before that, of an infection he received from one of his patients during surgery. How often and how hard I wished he had been able to care for Mamma when she became ill, for I am sure he could have made her well. Dr. Charles Gregory Leigh (that, of course, is where Derek gets most of his name—the Derek was just because Mamma thought it strong and manly) was looked up to by all his patients and by the other physicians with whom he worked.

Another crash! That one seemed directly over the roof, but I felt no impact, so I assume I am still alive.

I recall one late afternoon, just a very few days before Mamma died. Derry and I sat by her bed, each of us holding one of her hands. Her beautiful dark blue eyes had become enormous and were sunk deep in her thin face. She turned to Derry.

"Derek, you must care for Rosemary, you know."

"Yes, Mamma, I know."

"You will take her back to America with you?"

"Must we talk about this, Mamma?" Derry's voice choked.

"Yes, son, we must. I need to know that all will be in proper order when I can no longer see to things myself. Will you take her back with you? Or stay here? The house will be yours, you know."

"I know. But I think I must go back to the States, at least for a while. Uncle William has invested a great deal of time and patience in teaching me the legal profession. I feel it would not be honorable to leave him now, when I am just becoming of use."

"You are right, Derek. We should all be grateful to William. He was the first of the family to go to

America, and he seems to have been successful there."

"He is, Mamma. He runs the Vicksburg office, and I work more and more with him on every case. He wanted very much to come home with me. You must know that. But it seemed impossible for both of us to leave. . . ."

"And as much as I love my brother, I would rather have you with me now, Derek. I am so proud of you! I believe that for young people, such as you and Rosemary, a new and rising country must offer a great deal. Opportunity, growth, a boundless future. I have missed you, son, but I have always been glad that you had the courage to go. And when you go back, you will take your sister."

"Yes, Mamma."

"Then that is settled." She sighed, but she smiled slightly. "I have heard the southern United States are quite beautiful. I have often thought I should like to see them."

"They are very different from England, Mamma. In fact, each of the states is different from the other. It is an enormous country! There will be much for Tad to see and learn."

Derek is the only one who calls me Tad. That is because he was a big boy of eight when I was born, and he was, I am sure, disappointed that I was not a brother. Papa told me that when Derry first saw me he stared, and then said, "I expect it's just as well, she's not a boy. She's just a little tad of a thing, isn't she, Papa?"

The nickname seemed lacking in dignity when I became six or so, and I asked Derry to call me by my real name. Then, of course, as older brothers will, he would tease me with nonsense rhymes, such as:

"Rosemary Monica Stafford Leigh
Lived at the top of a tamarack tree.
The wind blew strong and the wind blew free
And toppled that towering tamarack tree
With Rosemary Monica Stafford Leigh,
Who fell kerplop and bloodied her knee."

"Who ever heard of a tamarack tree," I said, hoping I sounded scornful. "You just made that up!"

"It's a larch tree, silly. In America they're called tamaracks. Uncle William told me. It's an Indian word and *I* like it! Tamarack! Tamarack! Tamarack! Baby sister Tad in a tamarack tree. She fell kerplop and bloodied her knee!"

I stomped off with what dignity I could muster, and thereafter settled for "Tad" as a name.

After Mamma died (that is still so hard for me to write!) Derek, with the aid of the family lawyer and several close and helpful friends, packed the things we decided to bring with us and closed the house. It is still his, and it is comforting to know we can go back to London anytime we choose.

Right now, for example! To be safe in London where there isn't a war going on!

1859

LONDON IS SO VERY FAR AWAY. IT TOOK WEEKS TO GET here. First the long, windy, biting cold voyage across the Atlantic with the ship rolling and rocking beneath our feet (though I must say with some satisfaction that I was one of the few who never experienced the rigors of *mal de mer*) until we finally arrived at New Orleans in the late summer of 1859. I could barely believe that such a place existed! Warm and sunny, virtually exploding with flowering shrubs and trees, blossoms and greenery spilling from containers fastened to the iron grillwork that adorns many of the houses. The streets seemed filled with Negroes, almost the first I had ever seen. In London one sometimes sees dark-skinned Indians, the women in their beautiful saris, but rarely people as dark as these were. Some were at the dock to unload the ship, their skin like polished ebony, shining with perspiration; some drove smart carriages, sitting very straight in the front while their white employers in the back protected themselves with parasols or wide straw hats; some were white-kerchiefed maids accompanying their mistresses on shopping expeditions. I was fascinated!

"Who—what—are they?" I asked Derry.

"Africans. Some are stevedores, some are house-servants, most are slaves."

I shivered. "What a dreadful word. Slaves!"

"You'll have to get used to it, Tad. You will hear it often."

"It has such an ugly sound. Like 'serf' or 'vassal.' But somehow worse."

Derry gave my arm a gentle squeeze, but said nothing more.

Everyone seemed friendly toward us. Many people spoke a French-English combination so oddly accented I found it difficult to understand; Creole, Derek explained, and taught me that in Louisiana there was also "creole" cooking, which he insisted we sample. I found it delicious, filled with mysterious ingredients such as a green vegetable called okra, and tiny little crabs. I had not realized this "new world" would be new in so many ways.

After two nights spent with a family named Lauture, friends of Uncle William's and law acquaintances of Derry's, we boarded a steam-driven stern-wheeler for the trip up the Mississippi River to Vicksburg. What strange names Americans find for places. Mississippi! It sounds like a sneeze!

The riverboat was a ponderous vessel, puffing a slow progress up the winding waterway. The river twists and turns upon itself and I am sure the trip could be taken directly by land in a quarter of the time the river demands. The days were slow and quiet and warm, and I often found myself half-asleep in a comfortable chair on the sunny deck. From time to time we stopped to take on freight or passengers, and always I saw the bales and bales of cotton stacked on the docks, awaiting transport. Between the towns I saw miles of cotton plantations, with Negroes working in the fields under the hot sun. Some of them would straighten up as the steamer went by, sometimes waving, at other times, just staring for a moment before bending again to their work. Fieldhands, Derry told me. I gazed after them for a long time.

At last we approached Vicksburg in the state of Mississippi. I stood at the rail with Derek, looking upward to the top of the high bluffs on which the city is built.

"Is it possible that people can *live* up there? Why don't they topple directly into the water?" I asked.

"Once you are on land, you will see it is not as precipitous as it looks. The city goes up rather like a flight of stairs."

"But with no banister to slide down," I said. "I don't think I want to live near the top."

"Don't be so certain. The view is magnificent."

As I now know. Though whether a view of shellfire and flames can rightly be called "magnificent" I am not sure.

As we came closer I could see that at the base of the bluffs were the docks and wharves and shipping establishments. More bales of cotton, crates of fruits and vegetables, Negroes ready to unload from our vessel the goods destined for Vicksburg and reload with goods headed farther north. It was busy and noisy, and exciting. Above river level, streets of shops and business houses appeared to be clinging determinedly to the side of the steep yellow clay incline, and above these were dwellings; smaller ones below, great impressive residences at the top.

"Where are we to live?" I asked.

"I don't know yet. The two rooms I had over the law office would hardly be adequate for both of us, but Uncle William promised to find us a place. He will be here to meet us, I know."

And there he was. Derek saw him before I did and pointed him out to me. A tall, broad-shouldered man, looking much like our mother, his sister: dark, thick hair, deep blue eyes, and a suntanned, friendly face. I waved, and he waved back. When my feet touched the mercifully unmoving landing place, he was there to take me into his arms.

"Rosemary! What a long time it has been! Let me look at you, child."

He stood back from me for a moment, and then put his arms around me again in a great hug.

"What an attractive young woman you have become! The best points of both your parents. Your mother's beautiful, clear skin, and eyes just like your father's, that same light golden brown." Then his voice dropped. "You have had a difficult time, Rosemary, I know. To lose both your parents ..."

I did not trust my voice to answer him, but I managed a wavering smile in gratitude for his sympathy.

"Have you been able to find us somewhere to live, Uncle?" Derek asked. "After traveling half across the world, Tad needs a place to settle down."

"I have rented a small house—I think you will approve. It is furnished rather scantily, I'm afraid, but well enough to be getting on with."

"We brought a few things," I said, "and I am sure we will be comfortable." I stared up at the steeply pitched city above us. "How do we get there?"

Uncle Will laughed. "You are probably expecting to climb up on your hands and knees, but it isn't that difficult. Come. I have a carriage waiting. Is your baggage all together?"

Derek indicated our pile of boxes, bags, trunks, and valises, and Uncle William beckoned to a tall, sturdy black man, who had seemingly been waiting.

"Can you get these things into the carriage, Hector? If there is too much the rest can come up later."

The man called Hector answered in a soft, deep, rumbling voice. "No trouble, Mr. Stafford. I'll get everything in with no trouble."

I watched him lift a heavy trunk onto his shoulder and walk to a large carriage. Immensely tall, with great smooth muscles, he stepped easily as if he felt no weight at all.

"Is he a slave?" I asked softly.

Uncle William laughed. "Certainly not. Hector is employed at our law office. He keeps the place clean, does errands for both of us—makes himself useful in a hundred ways."

"We'd never manage without Hector," Derry added, "and he is as free as you or I."

I sighed with relief and followed the men to the carriage.

It seemed impossible that our vehicle could ever ascend the appalling uphill grade of the street, even with two sturdy horses pulling it, but Uncle William pointed out to me a sort of crosswise ladderwork of stones and bricks which enabled the horses to set their feet firmly. Plank sidewalks edged the streets, helping to keep pedestrians' feet from the mud. We crossed several roads and then turned right, passing rows of small, neat houses, many of them with garden plots of flowers or vegetables. The carriage drew up before one gateway, and I gazed with approval at a tidy little white wooden house with a low picket fence around the yard. Green shutters framed the windows which looked down the bluff to the river.

"This is it," Uncle Will said. "Do you think it will do?"

"Admirably," Derry replied.

I was enchanted. "It looks like an oversized dollhouse," I said. "It's perfect!"

Uncle William fitted a key into the lock of the front door as Derek and I stood beside him, and Hector began unloading our bags. When the door opened I walked into a tiny hallway that led to a small parlor, through that to an even smaller dining room, and then to an ample kitchen. Everything was spotlessly clean, and the furniture was more than adequate. What fun I shall have taking care of it, I thought.

"There are two bedrooms upstairs," Uncle William said, "and I have taken the liberty of engaging a cook and housekeeper for you." He grinned at me. "Don't worry, Rosemary. Amanda is not a slave and never has been. She will have her little girl with her during the day, and will go home in the evenings. I hope that is agreeable."

"I don't know what I shall do with a servant in this sweet little house, but it was kind of you to think of it, Uncle. Where did you find her?"

"She is Hector's wife. I told you Hector is invaluable in many ways. And you do need her, even if you don't think so. With Derek rising rapidly in the legal profession you must live as a 'lady' does, even if it is on a smaller scale."

I smiled. "Very well," I said. "I shall try to behave like a proper lady of the manor. Thank you."

After Uncle William left I explored the house and then began unpacking our belongings. As I hung my clothes in the wardrobe upstairs and set a few favorite ornaments around, the house began to seem more our own. I must have started humming with pleasure because Derry stopped me on the stairs.

"You sound happier than in weeks, Tad."

"I am. It's so nice to get settled in one spot. And such a cozy spot!"

A few minutes later there was a gentle rapping on the outer door of the kitchen and I ran to answer it. There stood a tall black woman, a white kerchief around her head, neatly and cleanly dressed. By the hand she held a small child, not more than three, I thought.

"Miss Rosemary?"

"Yes. You must be Amanda. Please come in."

As the woman stepped through the door with a beautiful dignity, the little girl stared shyly up at me from large brown eyes. Her thumb was in her mouth.

"This is my daughter, Betsy," Amanda said. "Betsy, say how do you do to Miss Rosemary."

The child pushed her thumb more securely into her mouth and stared at me unblinkingly. Her mother shook her shoulder lightly. "Betsy! Where are your manners?"

Removing the thumb, Betsy pressed her face against her mother's full skirts. I could barely hear her whisper "Howdydo, Miss Romy."

"Betsy will be no trouble to you, Miss Rosemary. I'll take care of her—keep her out of your way."

"You don't need to, Amanda. I like children, and she is lovely. I am so glad you are here. America is all new to me, and there is so much I must learn—about shopping, and where to find things, and so on. You will need to teach me."

"Don't you fret, Miss Rosemary," she said. "We'll do fine together. Just fine."

She opened a bag she carried, pulled out a white apron, and tied it about her firm waist. Then she reached into the bag again and removed several small parcels.

"I fetched a few things from the market," she said. "I'll fix a little something to eat, and we'll go to the shops after that."

"Oh, thank you, Amanda. I'll finish unpacking. Call us when lunch is ready."

Soon after luncheon there came the sound of the brass knocker on our front door. Derek and I had finally un-

packed the last piece of luggage and he had gone outside to inspect our tiny backyard. I was in the parlor
with an armload of books to place on the shelves that
flanked the fireplace. My hair was coming loose from
the ribbon that had held it back while I worked, I had
borrowed an apron from Amanda to cover my wrinkled
frock, I had removed my hoop and two of my petticoats, and my face and hands were smudged. I was
about to put down the books and answer the door when
Amanda appeared from the kitchen.

"Get yourself upstairs, Miss Rosemary, and tidy up
a mite. That's visitors at the door. I saw them coming.
Run now."

I dropped the books and ran. Visitors! Good heavens! If they saw me now they would never call again,
whoever they were. As I washed my face and hands
with cool water from the pitcher on my washstand, I
could hear light female voices from downstairs, with
Amanda's deeper voice speaking quietly. I snatched
off my trailing hair ribbon and tried to pull a comb
through my thick dark hair (so like Mamma's), with
only mediocre results. I untied the apron, smoothed my
dress as well as I could, took a deep breath, and walked
sedately down the narrow stairs.

As I entered the parlor, Amanda was setting the last
book in place on the shelves. A girl of about my own
age was seated there with a woman who was undoubtedly her mother. Amanda threw me a quick glance of
inspection, nodded her head slightly, and left the room.
I stopped just inside the doorway.

"I'm Rosemary Leigh," I said.

The older woman rose. "And how glad you must be to have arrived at last," she said. "I'm Mrs. Edmund Blair, and this is my daughter ..."

The girl bounced to her feet and came quickly to me, holding out both hands. "I'm Mary Byrd Blair," she said, and smiled. The way she pronounced her name made it sound like "Murburd Blaiyuh," but the boat trip up the river had somewhat accustomed me to the soft, slurring Southern speech.

"How nice of you to call," I said. "Do sit down. How did you know we were here?"

"Your uncle, William Stafford, is a good friend of ours," Mrs. Blair said. "As a matter of fact, I believe I was of some small help in locating this house for you and your brother."

"It is a charming little house," I said. "I have been trying to unpack and put away our belongings—I hope you will forgive my appearance...."

"Oh, pshaw," Mary Byrd said. "Don't you fret yourself about a little thing like that. We just met your uncle down on Washington Street and he told us you were here, and I said to Mamma, 'Let's us just drop in and say hello and be neighborly, 'cause after all they have come all the way from England and that poor girl won't know a single soul here and I can't bear to think of her being lonely,' and Mamma said, 'Not on the very first day,' and I said, 'That's just the right time,' and so we came." She beamed at me.

"I'm so glad you did," I said. And I was! I had not realized how much I needed to *know* someone in this new place. That was when Amanda entered quietly

from the kitchen, carrying a tray with three glasses
and a small plate. It was as though we had known
guests were coming and were prepared! As the glasses,
filled with a cool fruit drink, were accepted, and the
plate of thin, crisp biscuits was passed, I looked more
closely at my first callers.

Mrs. Blair was a short, plump woman with a happy,
unlined face, and I liked her immediately. She sat erect
on the edge of her chair (I was sure she was so tightly
corseted that she could sit no other way) and her mod-
erate hoop held out a gray chambray dress with soft
falls of white lace at throat and wrists. She wore a
jaunty little bonnet of matching gray with a lace frill
beneath the brim that framed her rosy face. A reticule
rested on her lap and a parasol leaned against her
chair. Her calm friendliness reminded me of my
mother.

Mary Byrd looked just like a doll I once cherished.
Her truly golden hair seemed to sparkle in the sun that
came in the parlor windows, and her clear blue eyes
were fringed with the most enviable long dark lashes.
The pink striped dimity frock and small pink bonnet
she wore made my own English schoolgirl clothing appear dreary by comparison, and made me yearn for
something more attractive. Perhaps Mary Byrd would
help me find some light, bright gowns like hers.

"What delicious cookies," Mrs. Blair said.

Cookies, I thought to myself. At home they are biscuits, but here they are cookies. I must remember.
"Thank you," I replied. "To be quite truthful I have no
idea where they materialized from. Uncle William

found Amanda for us, and I am beginning to think she must be something of a magician."

"Then be grateful, my dear. She can be of enormous help to you."

"Rosemary," Mary Byrd broke in, "I may call you Rosemary, may I not? And I just want to say right now this minute that Mamma and I are so *very* sorry about *your* mamma, but I think we won't go on talking about it because now that you are here and by way of starting a new life for yourselves, it's just better to put the dark things behind you and go on all brand-new, and I think we are going to be just the *closest* friends!"

She stopped for breath, and as she took a sip of her drink I heard Derry's voice in the kitchen. A moment later he came into the parlor.

"Derry," I said, "we have guests. Mrs. Blair, Mary Byrd, this is my brother, Derek Leigh. They are friends of Uncle Will's, Derry, and were kind enough to call on us."

Derek bowed over each lady's hand. "Mrs. Blair," he said. "Miss Blair."

Mary Byrd's eyes widened and then the dark lashes fluttered most effectively. I wished I could do that but knew I'd look ridiculous.

"Uncle Will has often mentioned you, Mrs. Blair," Derry went on. "In fact he has even suggested I accompany him to call upon you."

The woman smiled. "And why didn't you, Mr. Leigh?"

Derek pulled a long face. "I am here to study law with my uncle, and he is a hard taskmaster." Then he smiled. "I do want very much to be of actual help to him in his practice. I hope you forgive me. The loss has been mine."

"Well, we will surely take care of that, Mr. Leigh," Mary Byrd broke in. "We'll plan all sorts of amusing things for Rosemary to do, and you must escort her. A dancing party, I think—don't you, Mamma?—so that Rosemary and her brother can meet our friends, 'cause I am just *sure* they are most competent dancers, or perhaps some games would be pleasant ... we'll plan something, won't we, Mamma? Of course we will!"

I saw Derry's eyes twinkle and he put his lips tight together, sucking in his cheeks a bit, as he does when he is trying to hide a smile, Mary Byrd *did* chatter.

Mrs. Blair set her empty glass down on a little table and rose.

"We must go, Mary Byrd, and let these young people get comfortably settled in their new home. I do hope we did not intrude too much on your very first day. My daughter can be quite determined on occasion, as you will doubtless learn."

Mary Byrd joined her mother as she moved toward the door. "I would most surely rather be determined than a wishy-washy female with the vapors," she said, and took my hand in both of hers. "Let's be friends, Rosemary. Real close friends!"

"I'd like that," I said.

"I'll be by again in a day or so," she promised with a last, long look at Derek, and then they left.

Derry closed the door quietly behind them and his dark eyebrows arched quizzically. "Quiet little thing, isn't she?" he said. "Not a word to say for herself. And she has all the fluttering graces."

" 'Fluttering graces'? What do you mean?"

"Didn't you see the long lashes modestly covering the wide eyes? The little swish of her skirts when she moved? I am sure she is adept with a fan and a parasol. Those are fluttering graces."

I sighed. "Do I have any? Fluttering graces?"

His eyebrows lifted in surprise. *"You,* Tad? No, thank heaven. You're just yourself, for which I am very grateful."

"Well, *I'm* not grateful," I said, more heatedly than I intended. "I'm tired of being stodgy, dependable Rosemary in her stodgy, practical clothes! And what a crock I'd be at a party! I can't even dance, Derry, I never learned!"

He gazed at me in astonishment for a moment, and then he put his arm across my shoulders. "Sometimes I forget you're growing up. Don't worry, Tad. Miss Blair was right on one count. I must admit I am a 'most competent dancer,' and I'll teach you all I know. Agreed?"

"Agreed," I said. My brother is such a comfort to me! He was correct about writing when I become upset, too. Thinking of that early quiet, pleasant time has helped to blot out some of the fear and strain of these last months. . . .

Just as I wrote those words—"the fear and the strain of these last months"—there came a most tremendous explosion outside the house and I could feel the heavy vibration. From the kitchen came shrieks and moans. I dropped my pen and fled through the dining room, nearly colliding with Betsy who was running toward me, screaming at the top of her lungs, her hands clasped to her forehead.

"I been kilt, Miss Romy! I been kilt!"

"You're not killed," I said, lifting her. "Where's your mamma?"

"She's kilt, too!"

Holding Betsy, I ran into the kitchen. Amanda was slumped in the rocking chair, her face ashen pale. "What is it?" I cried. "Are you all right, Amanda?"

She nodded slowly, and waved one hand toward the far wall of the kitchen. A hole had been torn in the outer wall by pieces of an exploded shell. They lay on the floor, mixed, unfortunately, with the contents of a stone jug of molasses which had been on the table.

I shook so much that I had to set Betsy on her feet. I clutched the edge of the table, my knees threatening to give way, my heart pounding. After a moment I steadied myself and took the deepest breath of which I was capable.

"Let me see your head, Betsy," I said. "Does it hurt?"

I gently pulled her hands away from her head, revealing a wide gash. Blood dripped down her cheek and she sobbed piteously. I wet a cloth and started cleaning the wound so I could see it better.

"Amanda, bring me some of that clean linen we put away to use as bandages. Come now, we're all right.

Betsy's head is not near as bad as it seems." I did so hope I was correct! The poor woman got to her feet, moaning softly. I could not blame her.

The wound was apparently the result of a small chip of the shell, which had struck Betsy with sufficient force to graze her forehead, but the cut was not deep. Under the application of the cold cloth the bleeding soon stopped. I smoothed an unguent over the cut and then tied a strip of linen rather rakishly around her head. It was obvious that a sizable lump was developing beside the wound, but I decided not to mention it.

"There," I said. "Now you can pretend you're a wounded soldier. Show your mother."

Pleased with so much attention, Betsy climbed onto Amanda's lap, Amanda having retreated back to her rocking chair.

"See, Ma? I'm a wounded soldier."

Amanda put her arms around the child, holding her close, and looked at me over the woolly black head with the startlingly white bandage.

"Thank you, Miss Rosemary," she said softly, and although her chin trembled, the words came out clearly. "We are all right now. I'll clean up that mess in just a minute or two."

I started to tell her not to bother, that I would take care of it, but then I realized that, just as taking care of Betsy's injury had helped me, having a task to perform would very likely help Amanda.

And so I left the kitchen and came back here to my

desk. And I sit here, the pen loose in my hand—a hand that is still shaking—and say to myself, You are in the middle of a war, Rosemary Leigh. Unlikely as it seems, you are in the middle of a most unpleasant war that is going to get much worse before—one way or another— it is over.

And I know I'm about to put my head down on my arms and weep.

1859-1860

I HAD NEVER TRULY UNDERSTOOD THE MEANING OF "social butterfly" until I met Mary Byrd. If there were young men about, she had a way of walking that reminded me of the legendary Pied Piper. When she turned her head a fraction toward them, one could almost see an invisible pipe brought to her lips, causing a line of Southern gentlemen to rise to their feet and follow her. Derek was right: she handled a fan as if she had been born with one in her baby fist. Her wide blue eyes would peer over it, glinting with admiration of whichever young man she was talking to—or listening to; for in spite of her frequent spurts of chatter, Mary Byrd could make any speaker feel she was utterly absorbed in whatever was said. Her light laugh was quick and ready for any clever—or even not so clever—remark, and somehow she could make a young man stand taller and regard himself as a very gay blade indeed. If to my British upbringing it seemed a pose, I soon learned that was not true. Mary Byrd's fluttering graces were as natural to her as breathing.

By contrast I must have appeared a clod. I was barely thirteen when Mamma first became ill, too old for children's parties, not quite old enough for "young people's" parties, and by my own choice stayed close to home and my mother. What mixed social life I might have had I refused, preferring to do whatever I could to ease my mother's pain, and to take over the running of our small household. The result was that I was competent at domestic skills, but shy and rather ill at ease with my contemporaries of either sex.

Mary Byrd soon attempted to change that. Derry and I were invited to the Blairs' beautiful house for small dances, to play cards or parlor games, to listen to music. Derek seemed very much at home, but I frequently lurked in corners until a determined Mary Byrd would bring me forth and insist that I become involved in whatever activity was in progress. Derek helped, dancing with me at home (to tunes hummed in his rather off-key voice), coaching me quietly in the silly games, standing at my shoulder when cards were played, ready to offer advice. Gradually I began to enjoy myself, knowing I owed these new pleasures to Mary Byrd's friendship.

We spent hours together. We went shopping in Washington Street, where Mrs. Blair accompanied us to choose materials for a few new dresses for me—"Something a little cooler for our warm weather, Rosemary dear. . . ." We went to the dressmaker's, where we pored over patterns until the perfect ones were finally agreed upon, returning time after time for fittings. Some afternoons we visited Clarke's Literary Depot to buy a book or periodical, then stopped at any one of a number of genteel cafés for a dish of delicious ice cream—there were many leisurely things to do.

At other times Mary Byrd and I simply talked. She wanted to know all I could tell her of life in London; I wanted to learn all she could teach me of life in America.

We sat one afternoon in her bedroom, the sun coming in through wide-open windows, the ruffled white curtains moving gently in the light breeze from the river. She had been trying on a new frock for my benefit, and now, having hung it back in her wardrobe, she sat cross-legged on her pink canopied bed as we talked. Dressed only in her corset, laced to make her small waist even smaller, her long drawers trimmed with delicate lace, her chemise, her underpetticoat, her white petticoat with three starched flounces, a final thin muslin petticoat, her lacy knitted stockings, and thin white slippers on her feet, she looked like a drift of white cloud that had settled.

Quite spontaneously a question popped out of me. "How do Southerners think of their slaves?"

The delicate brows arched in surprise. "Why, we all *love* our people, Rosemary. Of course I don't see much of ours; they're way out on our plantation at Champion Hill. But my daddy builds cabins for them, and he says they sing while they're working, and they're happy folks! Whatever would they do if we didn't look out for them? I know Northerners think it's wrong to have slaves, but they don't understand how it is in the South. The slaves and the plantation owners—well, they need each other to get along. It's like children, my daddy says. Parents see after their children, but the children must do as they're told."

"But the children grow up and become parents," I

pointed out to her. "The slaves don't become masters."

Mary Byrd patted my hand. "Don't worry your head about it, sugar," she said. "It's just the way things are in the South. The way they'll always be."

I told Derek of this conversation. "What do you think?" I asked. "You have lived here for four years now. You must have opinions of your own."

"Of course I do. But they are the opinions of an outsider, a foreigner—not an American."

"Please tell me. I need to understand—if that is possible."

"Very well, Tad." He got up from the little sofa and clasping his hands behind his back, walked once or twice across the room, before turning to me. "In the four years since I came here I have observed the business of slavery carefully. You must keep in mind that in the northern part of America there is a large amount of industry and commerce. There are factories that employ workers, there are business establishments, and an enormous shipping trade. Here in the South, because of the climate, far and away the majority of people are engaged in some form of agriculture. They plant cotton or tobacco or sugar or coffee or any of a number of crops, and since Negroes are able to withstand the intense heat—because of their African heritage—they make good field hands. If a plantation owner is to achieve wealth from his crops—and isn't that a natural goal?—he expands by buying more land and then more slaves to increase production. From the owner's point of view, is that so wrong?"

"From *my* point of view it is wrong to own people," I said flatly. "For any reason! We British would never do that."

Derry gave me a half-smile. "Tad, 'we British' were not only slave owners but also slave traders until about thirty years ago."

I stared at him. "I don't believe it! Not the English!"

"Slave trading is a business like any other. It makes money. And there were no laws against it. Slavery is as old as time. There were slaves in all the British colonies and in most other countries at one period or another. White slaves as well as black."

I shook my head as if that would clear it and looked down at my tightly clenched hands. "But to *own* people," I said softly. "It cannot be right to own *people.*"

Derek came back to the sofa and sat down, leaning toward me, his arms resting on his knees. "That is the way the northern part of the United Sates feels: that it is wrong to buy or sell human beings; that if anyone, black or white, works for a living he should be paid for his work, just as we pay Amanda. And there you have the two sides of the slavery coin, Tad. The North feeling it is exploiting people who have no choice, the South considering it natural and desirable."

"But how do the slaves themselves feel?" I asked, looking at him.

He gave me his half-smile. "I doubt anyone has ever asked them, but I suppose it would depend largely on their masters. Some planters are intelligent enough to know that humane treatment of their slaves—decent housing and food and medical care—will increase their crops. Such owners treat their slaves rather like good horses. However, just like a horse, a slave may sometimes be whipped. And, as with animals, an owner may choose to keep one or two members of a family and sell the rest, just as he might keep the promising pups in a litter, and dispose of the runts."

"That's—that's heartless!" I flounced out of my chair.

"Perhaps. But try to remember there are probably more kind, protective slave owners than those who command by cruelty. It is to their advantage to be so. And remember, too, Tad, that very few free Negroes have enough education to support themselves. They must take whatever lowly work they can get, and live with less security than many slaves do. Is that any better?"

I had no answer. I walked to the window and stared out at the dark night. Derry's face was reflected in the glass and I could see him looking at me, a hint of sadness in his eyes.

"Since we came here," I said at last, "I have thought the South was so beautiful, so warm and welcoming and friendly. But now—now it's like ... like seeing a perfect shining stone in the woods and picking it up to find ugly worms on the underside. I cannot understand it all."

Derek appeared beside me in the window glass and I felt his arm across my shoulders. "Neither of us can really understand the Southern point of view," he said. "And so many of life's problems are caused by a lack of understanding and communication."

He is doubtless right, I thought. He generally is. But the knowledge doesn't clarify my mind about slavery.

When Derek and I first arrived in Vicksburg there was so much for me to see and learn that I was insensible of the emotional undercurrents around me. As 1860 wore on, however, I could not help but be aware of the strong feeling against a man named Abraham Lincoln, who had placed himself as a candidate for the presidency of the United States. I began reading *The Citizen,* a fairly reliable newspaper edited by Mr. James Swords. It contained articles about Mr. Lincoln with sketches showing a tremendously tall, big-nosed, gangling man. *The Citizen* described him as outspoken in his firm position against slavery, and referred to him as a Black Republican candidate, or Abolitionist. I thought him a striking figure and, in my usual blunt way, would have said so to everyone. Derek warned me.

"Remember where you are, Tad—in the midst of a city that is dead set against everything Lincoln stands for. In addition, you and I are not Americans. It behooves us to keep our mouths shut about our personal beliefs."

"But that seems dishonest! If everyone else can say what they think, why can't we?"

"No one asked us to come to Vicksburg. Neither of us knows whether we will stay here. If we take a stand in opposition to those who have made us welcome—well, as feelings get hotter, which they will, we could find ourselves quite unacceptable."

"Oh, that's ridiculous surely! You mean Mary Byrd would turn against me? Or—even less likely—against *you*? You are quite her ideal man."

"That's as may be. Mary Byrd is an engaging, frivolous child, and I am glad you have her as a friend, Tad. But if you openly declare yourself to be against everything she believes in—has been taught to believe in— she will find it difficult to preserve that friendship. You know that several states are considering secession from the nation because of the differences of opinion regarding slavery. They talk of forming a Confederation of Southern States, which would have nothing to do with the North. If a country can tear itself in half over the beliefs of its people, then certainly neighbors and friends and possibly even families can be split. Mind your tongue, Tad. Mind your tongue."

It was not easy. When, in the fall of 1860, Mr. Lincoln defeated three other candidates, including John Breckenridge, a proud son of the South, I wanted to cheer. *President* Lincoln, indeed! Now things would be set right, I was sure.

How blind I was. On the twentieth day of December, 1860, South Carolina seceded from the Union, followed by Alabama, Florida, Texas, Georgia, Louisiana, and Mississippi, and the Confederation of Southern States was formed, just as Derek had said, with Jefferson Davis as its president. Then President Lincoln was inaugurated and promptly announced that federal property in the southern states must be protected, especially the forts in the harbor of Charleston, South

Carolina. Fort Sumter was apparently the most important; a Northern officer, Major Robert Anderson, was ordered to take it from Southern General Beauregard. I tried to make sense of the battle from the reports in *The Citizen*, but it was not easy. After thirty-four hours of continuous gunfire from Beauregard in April 1861, Major Anderson retreated with "the honors of war." No one had been killed, but there remained no doubt as to how heated feelings had become. A new Confederate flag had been created (so much like the Union flag with its stars and bars that it was later the source of great confusion on a battlefield) and it was proudly hoisted to the top of Fort Sumter. The South rejoiced, and my mind was in utter confusion.

The next day I read in *The Citizen* that the "Black Abolitionist President Lincoln" had ordered troops to be used against all the seceding states, and that in a thumb-your-nose gesture the first seven had been joined by Arkansas, North Carolina, Virginia, and Tennessee—names I had barely heard of. Troops, I thought. Soldiers. Soldiers were for fighting, and fighting meant war. Yet all about me I heard the people of Vicksburg saying that there might be a few skirmishes here and there, but that nothing could ever harm their city. It was unassailable. Impregnable.

Those empty, foolish, comforting words!

April 1861

I BEGAN TO LOVE VICKSBURG. ITS FRIENDLY PEOPLE, its unhurried air, its now-familiar shops. I had Mary Byrd as a friend, and through her I met other young people. I was a trifle younger than most of them, but everyone was kind and thoughtful to me, and I was included in most of the social activities that went on. But it was not until I met Jeffrey Howard that I felt like a special person in my own right.

Jeff!

It was the evening of my sixteenth birthday and Derry had invited Uncle Will to dine with us. I was sitting in our little parlor waiting for them, wearing a new frock with countless petticoats which belled the skirt out gracefully. Creamy yellow organdy, the wide neckline baring my shoulders, the dress pleased me immensely. I had no great skill in doing my hair, so it was simply brushed until it shone like dark satin, and tied back with a yellow velvet ribbon. All in all I felt quite grown-up, and gratifyingly attractive.

When the door opened to admit the men I put down my embroidery and looked up, smiling. Uncle Will entered first.

"Good evening, Rosemary. How charming you look!"

"Thank you," I said, my eyes flicking past my uncle to the person standing a step or two behind him.

"I have brought you a birthday present," Uncle Will

went on. "This is Jeffrey Howard. He comes from Boston, in Massachusetts, and he knows no one in Vicksburg. I hope you will take him under your wing."

"It will be a pleasure," I said, rising and moving forward, and I never meant any words more sincerely.

He was several inches taller than I, and muscularly built. Smooth straight hair almost as dark as mine, the deepest brown eyes I had ever seen, and a handsome, unsmiling face. I thought he could not be more than eighteen. He took my hand and bowed slightly.

"Miss Leigh," he murmured.

Derry followed the other two men into the room, gave me a quick kiss on the cheek, said "Happy Birthday," and disappeared in the direction of the kitchen with a parcel under his arm. Slightly flustered by the unexpected guest, I rallied myself and tried to behave like a seasoned hostess.

"Do sit down," I said. "The evening is quite warm, isn't it?" I looked directly at Mr. Howard as I spoke.

"A welcome change after Massachusetts weather," he said quietly.

"Oh, I am so glad," I babbled. "I mean I am pleased that you find it welcome. When we first came to Vicksburg it seemed dreadfully warm to me most of the time. After England, you know." I stopped. It was always safe to talk about the weather. I had been taught that years ago. But what a ridiculous conversation!

Uncle Will rescued me. "Jeff is visiting me for a few weeks during his holidays from Harvard University," he said easily. "His father and I are law acquaintances, and I have known Jeff for years. It would be kind of you to show him a bit of the city while he is here."

"I shall be delighted," I said. I widened my eyes slightly as I had seen Mary Byrd do. "Are you enjoying your studies at Harvard?"

"As much as anyone ever actually enjoys studying," he said.

He certainly didn't give me much assistance in making light conversation! I was relieved when Derry came back into the room.

"I told Amanda we would be one more for dinner," he said. "She says it will be ready in fifteen minutes, if that is convenient."

"Perfectly," I replied.

My brother sat beside me on the small sofa, putting one arm across the back. "And how does it feel to have reached the ripe old age of sixteen?" he asked.

Blast Derek! Just when I was trying so hard to appear older! What interest would a college man have in a child of sixteen? I lifted my chin.

"If such pleasant company is the result, then I find sixteen to be delightful," I said, and felt rather proud of myself.

Derry laughed. "Good Lord! You are growing up!" He reached into his pocket and brought out a long flat box. "Happy birthday, Tad," he said, and handed it to me.

"Am I to open it now?"

"Please do. I think Uncle Will would like to see it."

I lifted the lid of the box and turned back a fold of

white silk. I am afraid my eyes and mouth opened wide with shock, for there lay a strand of small, beautifully matched pearls.

"Derry!" I slipped my fingers into the circlet and lifted it from its silken nest. The pearls seemed to glow in my hand.

"Do you recognize them?" Derek asked.

"No. Wait—were they Mamma's?"

"They were indeed. She gave them to me before ... that is, she asked me to give them to you on your sixteenth birthday."

Uncle William leaned forward, looking at the necklace as it swung from my fingers. "I remember," he said. "Our father gave them to her on her sixteenth birthday. Being some years younger, and a boy, I could not understand her pleasure. It seemed to me that a horse or a bow and arrow or some such practical thing would be a better gift."

I could feel tears stinging my eyes, and I wished Derek had waited until later. I was not about to weep like an infant in front of Mr. Howard. Dear Uncle William! Perhaps he guessed.

"Stand up, Rosemary, and turn around. I should like to fasten them on for you."

With my back turned toward the young man I blinked rapidly, swallowed a few times, and regained my control. When I faced him again, I could smile.

"Thank you, Uncle William, and thank you, Derry, for keeping them for me. It is the nicest present I could possibly have." With a new confidence I took a step toward Mr. Howard, my hand touching the pearls. "Are they not lovely?" I asked happily.

"Beautiful," he said, but he was looking straight into my eyes, and not at the necklace.

Amanda had prepared a memorable dinner and Derry's parcel had contained a bottle of some delicious golden wine, so that the evening became very festive. I discovered that Mr. Howard could most certainly smile in a fascinating way. His smile started in his dark eyes and then tipped up the corners of his mouth. At last, with a beautiful birthday cake before me, Uncle Will insisted I make a wish before I blew out the candles.

"Tonight there seems little to wish for," I said.

"There must be something."

"Well, then I wish that I may spend every birthday in company as warm and welcoming as this."

Ceremoniously Mr. Howard rose, lifting his wineglass. "I propose a toast," he said, "to Miss Rosemary Leigh, the most charming hostess it has ever been my pleasure to meet."

"Hear, hear," said Uncle Will, and immediately he and Derek were on their feet, glasses raised, and their eyes upon me. I had not been so happy in a long time. I am sure I blushed.

With the sumptuous cake came two more presents. From Derek a beautiful little gold ring set with one lovely pearl to match my necklace, and from Uncle Will a small, perfect watercolor of Kensington Gardens in London, where I had so often played as a child.

"As your mother and I did, too," he said, when I told him. "I don't want you to forget where you came from, Rosemary. Be happy here, but remember London."

"I will," I promised. "Always."

There was one more surprise before that evening ended. We sat in the parlor after dinner, with the last of the sunlight shafting through the windows, when the knocker sounded, and Derek opened the door. Mary Byrd stood there, her lovely hair catching the golden gleam, her eyes bright.

"I just couldn't let Rosemary's birthday go by without seeing her for at least a little minute," she said.

"Come in, Mary Byrd." Derek stepped back to let her pass. "You know Uncle Will, of course ..."

She flashed her wide smile, and held out one slim hand. "Mr. Stafford ..."

Our uncle lifted her hand, touching it with his lips, before turning her lightly toward Mr. Howard.

"And this is a young friend of mine, Jeffrey Howard. He is visiting from Boston."

Again the smile and the offered hand, which Jeffrey Howard bowed slightly over, but I noticed he did not kiss it as Uncle Will had.

"From Boston!" said Mary Byrd, making it sound farther away than the moon. "Goodness me! All that way! I just don't think I ever met anyone from Boston before, Mr. Howard. You must tell me every single thing about it. What the people are like, and what sort of things they do, and just everything!"

I could see the small glint in the young man's eyes,

but his face and voice were perfectly serious as he replied.

"The people are much the same as here, Miss Blair. Two arms and legs, two eyes and ears, and one of everything else. By and large they eat, sleep, and converse—using the same language—as the people of Vicksburg. There really is not a great deal to tell."

Mary Byrd was silent a moment, and then a grin of sheer mischief lighted her face. "Touché, Mr. Howard," she said. "I am quite properly put in my place. But I do hope you will allow me the opportunity to introduce you to some young friends of mine who may have better manners than I. They will relish your quiet wit as much as I do." She turned quickly to me, her eyes twinkling. "A small birthday gift for you, Rosemary honey. I hope Derek will approve." She handed me a covered wicker basket that seemed to move alarmingly as I took it.

"What in the world . . ." I began, and again felt the basket move in my hands. Cautiously I lifted the top slightly and peered in. Two bright eyes met mine, and a small brown furry head pushed the lid higher. "A puppy!" I exclaimed. "Oh, the darling! Look at him, Derry—did you ever see anything so dear?"

Derek looked over my shoulder as I lifted the warm, wriggling little creature from the basket. "As a good Englishman I must approve of dogs," he said. "Is it anything in particular?"

"Not yet, but he will be. And very good of his kind, too. I'll let you find out for yourselves as he grows."

"What's his name?" I asked, holding the puppy up so I could look at his droll little face. He opened his pink mouth and gave a tiny bark. For the first time I heard Mr. Howard laugh.

"He just told you his name," he said. "His name is Woof."

And, of course, Woof he remained.

Mary Byrd left a moment or two later, and not long after that Uncle William and Mr. Howard took their leave as well. As we closed the door behind them I looked at Derek.

"This has been the very nicest birthday I ever had," I said. "Thank you for helping it to happen." Cradling Woof in one arm, I hugged my brother tightly with the other. He put his arm around my shoulders and held me close.

"Little sister," he said, "I am glad it has been happy for you. Sleep well."

June 1861

SUMMER IN MISSISSIPPI IS VERY HOT INDEED! I HAD thought that London summers were often overly warm, but never like this.

One evening in mid-June Uncle Will had dined with us—he frequently did; although he considers himself a passable cook, he said Amanda could "brew rings around him"—and then we took chairs out onto our small front lawn to catch what breeze there might be. The first stars were just pricking through the darkening sky. Derry and Uncle William had removed their jackets and I was plying my fan, which Mary Byrd had been teaching me to use properly. ("No need to blow up a gale with it, Rosemary! Just gently. So.") I could hear Amanda in the kitchen, and the clink of china and glassware accompanied by her soft singing as she washed the dishes.

"I am so grateful to you for finding Amanda for us, Uncle Will. It seems I learn something new from her every day. Meats here are often cut differently and have different names than in London. There are so many fruits and vegetables here I never saw at home. You must have known I'd need a lot of guidance."

He smiled. "It did seem providential when Hector remarked one day that Amanda's employers were moving from the state. I was just in time to engage her before she found work elsewhere."

"You always land butter side up, Uncle," Derek said

with a chuckle. "Things always work out right for you."

"That's because I lead such a blameless life."

"Blameless?" Derek raised one eyebrow. "I can think of at least one of your activities that might not be termed blameless."

Uncle Will looked mystified. "My activities?" Then he frowned slightly.

"You forget yourself, Derek. There is ... a lady present."

"Only Tad, Uncle."

"Precisely."

"What are you talking about?" I asked. "What on earth can't you discuss when I am present?"

Just then the front gate clicked open and we could see Hector's massive form silhouetted against the sky. Uncle Will greeted him.

"Ah, Hector. Good evening."

"Evening." He touched the brim of the broad straw hat he wore.

"Come to take your family home?" Derek asked.

"That's right. It's a nice night for us to walk together."

"Amanda should be about finished in the kitchen," I told him. "She prepared another wonderful meal for us tonight. Where did she learn to cook so well?"

"Just came by it natural, I expect." He patted his firm belly and laughed. Hector's laugh seems to come from a deep cavern somewhere. "There are times I wish she didn't cook so good. She's aiming to make a mountain out of me."

Amanda and Betsy came around the side of the

house, the child's small hand safely in her mother's.

"That was a superb meal you served us tonight," Uncle William told her.

"Thank you, Mr. Stafford. Cooking for folks who enjoy their food is a real pleasure. We'll see you tomorrow, Miss Rosemary."

"Yes, Amanda. Good night. Good night, Betsy."

Betsy gave us her sweet shy smile. "Night, Miss Romy."

We watched them as they walked through the gate and started along the road. The moon had come out and silvered their dark skin as they moved away.

"Has Hector worked for you long, Uncle Will?" I asked idly.

"About eight years, I think. Why?"

"Just interested. I never knew any Negroes before I came here."

"They are an interesting couple. Amanda's parents were slaves, and when they were quite young their owner died, giving all his slaves their freedom, their cabins, and small plots of land. Amanda was born a year or two later, so she has always been free. She and Hector manage very well, with both of them working."

"Was Hector *ever* a slave?" I asked.

"No. He was born in Liberia and came to America as a young man. And an exceptional man he is." He rose and stretched, picking up his jacket from the back of his chair. "And I must be off. Thank you both for another pleasant evening. I'll see you in the morning, Derek—"

"Yes, Uncle."

"And good night, Rosemary. You might ask Hector himself about his history. It's an unusual one that he dares not speak of to many people."

Uncle Will kissed my cheek lightly, clicked the gate shut behind him, and disappeared in the soft, dark night. We could hear him whistling.

"Where is Liberia, Derry?" I asked.

"On the west coast of Africa, and it's time for bed." Derek yawned widely. "Hold the front door open and I'll bring the chairs in."

In bed I wondered drowsily for a few moments about those strange few words between Uncle Will and Derry. "You forget yourself ... there is a lady present." But I fell asleep very quickly.

July 1861

THE "FEW WEEKS" THAT UNCLE WILLIAM HAD MEN-
tioned as the length of Jeffrey Howard's visit stretched
into months, and I couldn't have been happier. Jeff
called upon me frequently. I would be walking Woof
and see him marching up the hill, his jacket slung over
his arm, his collar loosened in the summer heat. As
soon as he saw me he would pull his cravat into place
and struggle into his coat.

"Jeff, there is no need to swelter on my account," I
told him.

"And no need for poor manners. Whatever will you
think of us Yankees if we don't know how to appear
before a female?"

"I've heard Yankees are noted for their common
sense. It makes no sense to dress in a warm climate as
you do in a cool one. Come inside and have a glass of
Amanda's lemonade."

Amanda's pleasure at being asked to provide re-
freshment, Woof's always enthusiastic greeting, and
my own (I am sure) obvious delight in seeing him succeeded in making Jeff feel welcome and at home. We
talked of all manner of things. One afternoon—it was
July, I remember, July 1861—Jeff arrived with a copy
of *The Citizen*.

"Have you read this?" he asked. "Your General
Beauregard has achieved quite a victory."

"Where? Doing what? And he isn't *my* general."

"Sorry. At Bull Run. Now don't tell me you don't know where Bull Run is."

"Certainly I know! It's near—um—Richmond. In Virginia. And Richmond is now the Confederate capital. See?" I gloated.

"Very good. We'll make an American of you yet. In any case, Pierre Gustave Toutant de Beauregard—Lord, what a name!—seems to have routed Union troops successfully, and has become a hero. You should be very proud."

"Proud! Jeff, don't tease me. I am no more a Southerner than you are! Yes, I live here, and I have made friends here, but I am *English*!" I looked straight into his deep brown eyes. "It is difficult sometimes."

"How, Rosemary?"

I rose and moved around the little parlor, trying to put my confused thoughts into some sort of order. "Since Derek brought me to Vicksburg," I said, "people have been so kind. Courteous—and helpful—and hospitable. They have made us feel liked—and *wanted*. Most of these people are slave owners. They buy and sell human beings like—like furniture! Perhaps, as I have been told, they are kind and caring to their ... property, but men and women are not property! Should not be! Must not be! Is it just because God gave some human beings black skin that white men do not regard them as *people*? Oh, Jeff, I don't know what to think! Sometimes I feel as if I were split right down the middle!"

He sat quietly, looking at me. Then he rose and came to where I stood by one of the front windows.

"Poor Rosemary," he said softly, and put his hand on my arm. "In the middle of somebody else's war."

"The War of Southern Independence," I said softly.

"In Boston, and in all the Union states, it is called the War of the Rebellion."

"Same war, different names. Strange, isn't it?" I turned and looked up at him. "You won't have to become involved, will you, Jeff?"

He was silent for a moment, and our eyes seemed locked together. "You know better than that," he said finally. "For my own personal pride, if for no other reason. This is just the beginning. Small battles and skirmishes here and there. But these will achieve momentum. It is like a huge rock rolling down a hill. It picks up speed slowly, but once it starts nothing can stop it until it crashes into whatever is at the bottom."

"And what is at the bottom of this hill, Jeff?"

"The South, I think, and its traditional way of life." He paused, and then said, "Did you ever read the American Declaration of Independence, Rosemary?"

I shook my head. "No."

"It was written more than a hundred years ago, when the thirteen colonies felt themselves unjustly used by King George the Third. There were many reasons, you can find them in any history book, and at last the colonists felt they must make their position and their aims totally clear. A man named Thomas Jefferson did the actual writing, putting into words what all the colonists believed and were struggling to attain. And some of his words are these: 'We hold these truths to be self-evident, that all men are created equal, that they are endowed by their Creator with certain inalienable rights, that among these are Life, Liberty and the pursuit of Happiness.' "

He stopped, but there had been something in his voice—a sincerity, a personal belief—that made tears spring to my eyes. "That's beautiful," I whispered.

"Yes."

"But what happened? Why does the South not feel that slaves should be free? Should have 'Liberty and the pursuit of Happiness'?"

"Perhaps the South feels that Negroes, most of them brought here from Africa through no wish of their own, are not 'men' as whites are 'men.' That equality has no meaning when applied to black men. That they are not truly Americans, and therefore do not have these rights."

"But that is ridiculous! A man is a *man*. A *person*. Does it matter where he comes from or what color he is? He is a human being, to be treated as one. Southerners are denying their own words, the words of their Declaration."

"Perhaps the North is, too. It is forbidding the South to live as it feels is right."

I felt a quick surge of anger and wheeled away from Jeff in a swirl of petticoats.

"Men behave just like children! Each side lays down rules—what do they call them?—ultimatums! They

say you *will* do this and you *won't* do that, and then
the other side—just like little boys!—says, 'Oh, no, we
won't,' or 'We certainly *will!*' And then they decide to
fight it out! Have a war! Kill each other!" I whirled
back to him. "Is *this* 'Life, Liberty and the pursuit of
Happiness'? Is it?"

"Rosemary, the economic structure of the South is
built on crops raised on plantations. Plantations which
must be supplied with enough manpower to produce
those crops. The South is not inflicting slavery on the
North, it is simply saying that if the South is to exist
and contribute financially to the rest of the nation,
slavery is an essential fact of life."

"Why can't they just *hire* men and *pay* them?"

"And thereby lose virtually all the profits of their
crops? Slavery has been in existence for hundreds and
hundreds of years. To Southerners it is the normal way
of life, something they have always known and expect
to go on knowing. I can understand this, but I do not
agree with it. And because I do not agree I must do
more than frown upon it. Can't you understand?"

"Of course you don't agree! Neither do I. But if
every two people who couldn't reach a friendly agree-
ment over an ... an issue rushed off to fight each
other—why, there would be nothing but war! Surely
this whole thing can be *talked* out."

"Not now, Rosemary. It's too late for that now. As I
see it I have no choice but to be willing to fight for what
I believe in."

I felt myself trembling with anger. How could he be
so stubborn? The idea of men imposing their will on

other men by killing them was senseless! If anything should happen to Jeff.... I felt my face was flaming and when I spoke my voice was too loud, but the words tumbled out.

"So you will go back to Boston and join the Union Army, I suppose, and then march bravely into Vicksburg and kill the friends you have made here!"

"I hope to God I never have to kill anyone," he said, and then his arms were around me and I could feel his warm cheek against my hair. "A man must be willing to protect what he thinks is right, and try to change what he thinks is wrong. I'm sorry, Rosemary. I'm so very sorry."

I wrenched away from him, trying desperately to hold back tears. "Then go back to Boston! Do whatever you like! And every time you have to kill someone just tell *them* how sorry you are!"

Leaving him standing there, I raced up the stairs and into my room, slamming the door behind me. A moment later I heard the front door close quietly and from my window I watched him walking away from the house, hands deep in his pockets, head down. Choking on sobs I threw myself across my bed and let the tears pour onto my pillow.

When Derek came home he told me Jeff was packing to leave for Boston. "I asked him to join us for dinner tonight so you could say goodbye to him, but he told me you already had."

"Yes," I answered. "I did. This afternoon."

And that was all.

Autumn and Winter 1861

LOOKING BACK TO THOSE MONTHS AFTER JEFF WENT away, I find it incredible that we lived as we did. Were we all truly blind or was it more comforting to hide our heads under the familiarity of our usual daily life? *The Citizen* told us of battles here and there, in places I had never heard of, and when the people of Vicksburg heard that the Confederates had won it was music to their ears. And I went shopping with Mary Byrd and Mrs. Blair and bought lengths of the plaid materials that had become so popular, hiring a Negro seamstress to make them up into dresses.

We read of a Virginian general named Robert E. Lee who rode victorious from one battlefield after another, and of a Northern general named Ulysses Simpson Grant—a name to make many of my young friends giggle, especially when it was pronounced "Useless"—and my interest followed General Grant and I could not admit it.

Derry went to the law office every day, where he and Uncle Will conducted business as usual, and there were parties where we became used to seeing young men in the gray uniform of the Confederate Army. The muted color provided an austere background for the bright frocks of the girls. And the conversation at these parties changed until the boys—for that is what most of them were—could talk of nothing but training and weapons, of strategy, and the battles to come, for which they were all eager. "One Southerner can lick six Yanks," they said. "Everybody knows that!"

An article in *The Citizen* said that President Lincoln and his advisors planned to split the South in half and cut both halves off from the North by controlling their source of trade and supplies, the Mississippi River. It was accompanied by a sketch showing a huge serpent in a Yankee uniform cap wrapping itself around the southern states and squeezing. This evoked great mirth from the young men. "Just let one of those cold-mouthed Northerners try to send a boat down the ole Mississip' and we'll stand up here and blow it to the bottom of the river!" they said. And, "Don't you sweet li'l ladies bother yourselves about Vicksburg, because there ain't nothin' can touch us!"

And I listened to their youthful boasting and did not speak. They were my friends. They had taken me in, had made me welcome in their city, had been kind to me, were fond of me. So I went to their parties and danced, and sang, and played games. I chattered and gossiped with Mary Byrd, planned meals and shopped with Amanda, and played with Woof. He was growing rapidly into a broad-chested dog with persuasive eyes and a harsh, wavy rusty-brown coat, against which I sometimes laid my face for comfort.

Christmas came and went with gifts and visiting and church and carols, and I received a greeting card signed "Always, Jeff." A silly message, I thought. Certainly he would always be Jeff. Who else would he be?

And why should I care what or where he was? He had gone away, paying no heed to my feelings. Still, I put the card at the bottom of my handkerchief box, and never quite forgot that it was there.

Uncle William and Derek and I sat in our little parlor one evening, talking. Amanda had provided one of her delicious meals, and she and Betsy had gone home. Woof was asleep, his head resting across my feet, and the two men and I were sipping tea, which we preferred to coffee. A fragile link with England, perhaps.

"Uncle," Derek asked, "do you think there is the slightest chance that Vicksburg could ever be taken?"

Uncle Will gazed into the teacup he held in two hands, savoring the fragrance. Presently he raised his dark blue eyes and looked directly at Derry.

"I think there is every chance," he said quietly.

"Surely not," I said flatly. "The city stands so high—how can we be reached?"

"By gunboats coming down the river."

"Those could be sunk by troops stationed above them."

"Rosemary, new ships are being built, iron-plated. What do you know of that can penetrate iron?"

A small cold feeling edged into my stomach. The thought of being in a beleaguered city was not attractive.

"Do you think I should send Tad somewhere else while travel is still possible?" Derry asked.

"And where do you propose to send me?" I snapped,

surprised at my own vehemence. "I know no one in this whole country except those I have met here! You two are the only people who belong to me! If you think for one misguided second, Derek Charles Gregory Leigh, that you are going to pack me off by myself to heaven knows where, you are quite wrong!"

Uncle William smiled. "I imagine that ends the discussion," he said.

Derry gazed at me, his lips pressed hard together. "For the moment, perhaps. But I intend to keep the thought in mind."

I went to bed with my head in a turmoil. My moral sense of right was with the North and its determination to rid the country of slavery and insurrection, but my heart was tied to Vicksburg. If the people here who had accepted me and were now my friends could withstand whatever might come, then so could I.

February-April 1862

By FEBRUARY OF 1862 THE NAME OF ULYSSES S. Grant was on everyone's lips, and the epithet "Useless" was rarely heard. He had scored a resounding Northern victory at Nashville, Tennessee, and the war moved a little closer to us. It was shockingly clear in the scarcity of trade on the river.

The beautiful spring came, and in April I had my seventeenth birthday. Three things that happened on that day stand out in my mind. I received a card, I had news of New Orleans, and I met Ben.

When Derry came home from the office he handed me a large white envelope.

"Uncle Will asked me to give you this," he said.

"What is it?"

"The best way to find out is to ..."

"I know! Open it. Very well."

I slit the envelope and drew out a card on which several small scenes had been drawn and watercolored. They were delightful! One showed the outside of our front door and the backs of three male figures standing there. I could identify one as Derry and one as Uncle Will, but the third I was not sure of. The next tiny picture was of a girl wearing a yellow organdy gown, and there was no doubt that she was meant to be me. There followed little sketches grouped together: a large birthday cake, its candles alight; a basket, the lid raised and a wee canine nose thrusting out; a raised hand holding a wineglass, and another—very feminine—hand lifting a string of pearls. My sixteenth birthday! Quickly I turned the card over. In the lower corner, exquisitely printed, the message: "Happy Birthday. Jeff." And below that, a tiny drawing of Jeff himself, wearing a Yankee uniform cap.

"Oh," I said involuntarily. "Oh dear!"

"Is something wrong, Tad?"

"No, not really. It's a card from Jeffrey Howard. He has joined the Union Army."

"That shouldn't surprise you."

"It doesn't actually. He told me he would. It's just—well, I was not precisely charming the last time I saw him. But look! See how cleverly he has drawn all these miniature pictures. And tinted them, too."

Looking carefully at the card, Derry smiled. "You must have made quite an impression, Tad. He hasn't forgotten a thing."

Especially me, I thought. He hasn't forgotten me. I was amazed at the comforting warmth the realization brought.

"How did the card get here?" I asked. "I thought mail was not coming through from the North."

"It isn't, or very rarely. Howard must have found some way to get this to Uncle Will." Tapping the card with his finger, Derek added, "The boy is truly an artist, isn't he?"

"Yes," I said, and slipped the card into the silk pouch I wore at my waist to hold my handkerchief. It felt warm against me.

"Now that you have had a pleasant remembrance,"

Derry said, "may I tell you some far less pleasant news?"

Surprised at the solemnity in his voice I looked up at him. "What?" I asked.

"New Orleans is close to being taken by Union troops."

"New *Orleans*?"

"Yes. Beautiful New Orleans will soon be a base for the Union Army."

"Oh, Derek! Tell me."

Feeling very unsteady, I sat on the edge of the little sofa. My brother roamed about the room, speaking in a disjointed way. "It's primarily a naval battle—there is a Northern admiral—his name is Farragut—do you recall Uncle Will talking about the ironclad ships? They are what are being used—the *Monitor* and the *Merrimack*—I don't remember the rest. The city is being bombarded—shelled—that beautiful city! So much of it destroyed!"

"It was the first place I saw in America. Such a lovely place!"

"Remember it as you saw it, Tad, for it may never be the same again."

"And you think it will be Vicksburg's turn next, don't you." I made it a statement, not a question.

"Not quite next. But sometime. It will happen sometime."

Presently we went in to dinner. Amanda had done her best to make it a festive meal, and Derry opened a bottle of wine and toasted me, but it was not the same as last year. When the birthday cake (a pathetically small one this year since certain cooking ingredients had become difficult to find) had been duly admired and eaten, we put Woof on his lead and went out for a stroll.

The evening was still, lightly scented with fresh growing things. Below us we could see the faint glimmers of light from windows, and other lights by the docks, reflecting in the river. It seemed so peaceful.

"It is hard to believe there is a war going on," I said softly. "How much longer will our world be as quiet as this, do you think?"

"I don't know, Tad. Not much longer, I'm afraid. Drink it in while you can."

Just then we heard the clip-clop of hooves on the dirt road and a moment later a buggy approached us, driven by a young man, with Mary Byrd sitting beside him. She raised her hand and hailed us.

"Happy birthday, Rosemary darlin'. I have brought someone to meet you."

Derek took the reins while the young man jumped down and held out his hand to assist Mary Byrd.

"This is my cousin Benjamin Blair Fraser and he lives way out at Champion Hill but he has come to town for a spell, and I told him he just had to ride along with me to wish you a happy birthday, 'cause he is just about the nicest cousin I have—even though I do have a great lot of them—so you treat him pretty, Rosemary."

Benjamin Blair Fraser took my hand and bowed

over it. "I wish you the happiest kind of birthday, Miss Rosemary Leigh," he said. He smiled at me, his gray-green eyes, framed in thick blond lashes, crinkling at the corners. His hair, slightly rumpled, was thick and taffy-colored, his nose was impudently snub, and his smile was wide. He had a happy, friendly, rather mischievous face, and I liked him immediately.

"Thank you," I said, and was just about to introduce Derek when Mary Byrd did so first.

"And this is Mr. Derek Leigh, Ben, and he is surely the most sophisticated man I ever met in my whole entire life, and I guess that comes from being English, don't you? Because the English are so much better educated than we little old Southerners are. . . ."

"Steady on, Mary Byrd," Derek broke in. "Don't be giving me so much to live up to. Happy to meet you, Mr. Fraser." The two men shook hands.

Mary Byrd stared at Woof, sitting politely beside me, his tail brushing joyfully back and forth across the dusty street.

"Lordy me," she said. "He has surely grown, hasn't he? He's a Chesapeake Bay duck dog, you know. Daddy has a whole mess of Chesapeakes out at the plantation. I must have told you that."

"No," said Derry, one dark eyebrow quirked, "you very carefully told us nothing."

"Oh. I reckon I was afraid you might not want him if you knew how big he'd get." Mary Byrd put out her hand and Woof licked it thoroughly, giving tiny whines of pleasure at the attention.

"Do you think it's safe to assume that he has stopped growing now?" Derry asked politely.

Mary Byrd flicked a glance up at him. "Oh, I should think so. You needn't bother yourself over Woof anymore."

Derek's voice was very quiet and his mouth had the shape it makes when he is trying not to grin. "And what should I bother myself over?"

Mary Byrd's eyes lifted to his, wide, innocent, and intensely blue. "Why, that's entirely up to you, Derek. Whomever—I mean *what*ever—you think is *worth* bothering about."

It was an odd little conversation that seemed to exclude the young man and me, and I felt I should be hospitable. "Won't you come into the house?" I asked. "There may be a crumb of birthday cake left, although I doubt it."

"Let's just walk a bit," Mary Byrd said. "It's such a pleasant evening. Tie the reins 'round something, Ben. The horse will stand."

While Benjamin Fraser fastened the reins loosely around a tree, Mary Byrd and Derek walked on ahead of us. In a moment Ben offered me his arm, I gave Woof's lead a little twitch, and we followed.

"You are living in Vicksburg now, Miss Leigh, or just visiting?"

"Derek and I live here—at least for the present. He is in our uncle's law office."

"And do you like it here?"

"Very much. The Blairs have been so very kind to

us, and Mary Byrd has introduced us to many new friends."

"I hope I will be counted as one of them."

"Certainly."

"You don't miss England?"

"Of course I do. London is home, and someday we will probably go back. But Derek's work is here, and both our parents are dead, so I should have been quite alone in England."

"I shall try to see that you are never alone here."

I glanced up at him to find him smiling down at me. He did seem a rather forward young man, but a pleasant one.

"And you are visiting the Blairs?" I asked.

"Yes. My family has a large cotton plantation just outside Champion Hill, and my father hopes I will stay and help him with it. But there is so much war talk—well, I thought I'd better get myself closer to the center of things and see what I could do to be useful."

"And have you found something useful to do?"

"I just guess I'd better enlist in the army and keep those Yankees out of our cotton."

I smiled. "All by yourself?"

"Oh, I'll accept help."

"Do you have slaves on your plantation, Mr. Fraser?"

"Ben."

"I beg your pardon?"

"My name is Benjamin, but everyone calls me Ben. I hope you will, too. Yes, of course we have slaves. Almost two hundred. How else could we raise cotton?"

"Two hundred!" I repeated, shocked. "You *own* two hundred people?"

"Own them, feed them, house them, see that they have medical care when it is needed, supply their clothing ... We even have a school for the children— try to teach them their ABCs, and how to write and figure a little. Other plantation owners think that is wrong, they feel a little education will make the Negroes uppity."

"I see," I said. I stopped beside a rail fence that ran along one side of the road, and leaned on it, looking down at the river.

"Are you against slavery, Miss Rosemary?"

"Yes, I am."

"I suppose it would be hard for anyone except a Southerner to understand it. And because of that lack of understanding, the states are at war." Suddenly he laughed, and his voice changed. "But what are we doing, squandering our first meeting on war talk! Does your offer of a possible crumb of cake still hold good?"

"If there is a crumb left, it is yours. Shall we catch up with my brother and Mary Byrd and go back to the house?"

"No. We will leave your brother and my cousin to their own rambling, and go back by ourselves. Woof will be your chaperone."

And then I laughed. "Woof's idea of chaperoning would be to climb into your lap and kiss you repeatedly on the face."

"Ah! If only Woof's mistress felt the same way!"

And laughing together at his nonsense, Ben Fraser and I turned and retraced our steps to the house. There was a very small slice of cake.

I think it must have been the early spring of '62 when I first began to *see* what was happening to our way of life—what the slowly strengthening blockade was doing to us.

In the shops along Washington Street, the great mounds of beautiful fresh fruit and vegetables dwindled. Dressmaking supplies, such as fabrics and trimmings, lace and buttons, feathers and flowers, were almost impossible to find. Building materials and books, medicines and paper, spices and soaps, all the many items we had taken for granted—everything brought in from the North or from Europe and shipped down the Mississippi—began to disappear. As stocks were used up there was no way to replace them.

And the great piles of cotton bales stood rotting on the docks. Just as nothing could be brought into the city, so nothing could leave it.

Still, there Vicksburg sat, high on the bluffs above the river, and everyone told everyone else that it could not possibly be taken. "An impregnable fortress," they said. "We could not be safer."

Young men assigned to different regiments kissed their mothers and sweethearts a gay goodbye and marched blithely off to "put an end to this inconvenience." And there were parties for them, and music, and laughter, and joking.

Ben Fraser seemed always to be laughing. He came calling on me to show off his new uniform. He looked particularly handsome in it, and I told him so.

"I must admit I consider it rather dashing myself," he said. "I shall be extremely careful not to muss nor soil it."

"Please do. You had best carry a clean handkerchief to spread on the ground should you become weary of marching and want to rest."

With mock solemnity, one eyebrow raised, he shook his head. "Oh, I shall never sit down. That might lead people to think I was tired, and a Confederate soldier would never admit weakness of any kind. Besides, sitting down might make wrinkles in my trousers."

I laughed. "It had better be a very short war if you are to remain standing stiffly at attention throughout, like a wooden soldier."

Suddenly he reached for my hand and held it tightly. When he spoke his voice had become deep and serious. "It had better be a very short war in any case," he said. "I never want you exposed to danger, Rosemary."

I stared at him, speechless. He had never made such a personal statement, and I must admit that it thrilled me. I wished I knew how Mary Byrd would have answered it.

But then Ben laughed again, gave my hand a squeeze, and said, "Put Woof's lead on and let's take a walk. I want everyone to see my new sartorial splendor."

As we walked I asked Ben questions about things I

had read in *The Citizen*. So many unfamiliar place names and war terms confused me.

"Tell me about the Western Flotilla," I said. "And about the River Defense Fleet. My mind is in a muddle."

"Very simple, my muddle-minded little British friend. In a war there are two sides. Do you understand that much?" I glared at him. "Good! We are making progress. So—in this particular war, the two sides are the South and the North. The North has created something they call the Western Flotilla, which they mistakenly assume will clear the Mississippi River of all Southern craft, taking town after town as they sail proudly along. This, of course, is sheer Northern vanity, since our Southern captain, James Montgomery, is the head of the River Defense Fleet. The two fleets met up north of here, somewhere between Cairo—that's Illinois, you know, not Egypt— and Memphis, which is in . . ."

"I know," I interrupted rudely, "that's in Tennessee. I *can* read a map, you know."

"How clever of you! Well then, Montgomery's fleet, using its rams—" He paused, looking at me inquiringly.

I nodded, trying not to look smug. "Rams. Of course. Vessels that have had their bows reshaped into pointed iron . . . beaks. Useful for hitting enemy boats amidships." I glanced up at him. His hazel eyes were filled with laughter.

"Extraordinary female! As I was saying, Captain

Montgomery rammed and sank the North's ironclad ship, the *Cincinnati,* and then reported firmly that the Western Flotilla would never penetrate farther down the Mississippi." He paused and made a wry face. "I suppose I should add that *after* that brave statement the North managed to batter Fort Pillow, close by Cairo, into a shambles."

"With their useless Western Flotilla?"

"Er—yes." He took my hand and swung it as we walked. "Anything else you would like explained?"

"I think not." We were silent for a moment, and then I said, "It is getting very close, isn't it, Ben? Not just on the river, but all around us."

"Yes, Rosemary, it is getting very close."

Almost in silence, we turned and went home.

Early May 1862

ONE LOVELY MAY MORNING, WHEN THE AIR WAS FRESH and still cool, Mary Byrd and I walked into the shopping area of the city. At least, it had been the shopping area.

"I need wool," she had stated. "I just don't know if I can find any, but we can look."

"Wool? What on earth for?"

"To knit socks for the soldiers, of course. Aren't you knitting socks for our brave boys?"

"It would take a lot of bravery to wear socks I knitted," I said. "I can sew rather well, but my knitting—well, best forget it."

"Oh, I don't knit very well, either, Rosemary. I do something very strange when I come to the heels. There seem to be a lot of bumps. But we have to knit, sugar. It's patriotic!"

I laughed. "There must be some way I can be patriotic without bumps. Any poor soldier who wore socks I made would be limping before he marched three yards."

"Then you knit them for Northern troops," she said lightly. "I just have to find wool somewhere."

We tried one shop after another without success, until we came to a tiny store tucked between two larger ones. In an immaculately clean window were a few goods laid out for display, including hanks of a particularly unpleasant purplish-colored wool. I pointed.

"There!" I joked. "Precisely what you need!"

"What luck! I'm going to buy all he has." She pushed open the door to the little shop.

"Mary Byrd! You're not going to knit purple socks!"

She looked over her shoulder at me, eyes wide with surprise. "Well, of course I am! Purple and gray are charming together!"

Laughing, I followed her in. The tired little man in the shop charged what we both felt was an exorbitant amount for the wool, but Mary Byrd paid it uncomplainingly. An additional skein was found, a horrid green that looked like bile, and she bought that, too. A few minutes later we left the store. I was still giggling.

"You could knit the socks in purple and the heels in green," I suggested. "That should brighten up those gray uniforms."

"Now don't you tease me, Rosemary. I believe in patriotism no matter what color it is!"

As we started to cross the road a procession of farm wagons deterred us. The first three or four were filled with soldiers, their neat uniforms clean and unstained. They waved and shouted at us as they passed.

"Where's this here war?" one called out. "We came specially to defend you young ladies, but we can't find any war."

"Where are you from?" Mary Byrd called back.

"Louisiana," one answered, and "Virginia," shouted another, while a third yelled, "Mississip'!"

We stood waving as they passed, calling greetings back and forth. But the next wagon to come along was different. It was filled with wounded. A few sat on the back of the wagon, swinging their feet; others lay quietly on piles of straw. I wanted to cover my eyes— even to me they looked so young! I started to turn away and could not. They wore soiled bandages on their heads, their arms, their legs. Their uniforms were torn and bloodied and grimed. Their faces were pale, though some still smiled and waved at us. Others lay silent, with closed eyes, and I wanted to hold my heart to keep it from breaking. In that slow, interminable procession there were five wagonloads of them and we watched until all had passed.

Neither of us spoke as we picked our way across the street, trying to avoid the horse droppings. I glanced at Mary Byrd. There were tears streaming down her cheeks. I reached out to grip her hand and held it tight.

Mary Byrd's hand squeezed mine, and then she drew it free to wipe the tears away.

"I just haven't seen any before," she said, her voice tremulous. "I guess I knew men were being hurt— wounded—but I hadn't seen them. It has all seemed like something that was happening somewhere else."

"I know," I said. And I did.

When Derry came home from the office that afternoon we sat in our little garden, having a watered-down cup of tea. Our supply of tea was nearly exhausted and neither Amanda nor I had been able to find more.

"Oh, by the by, Tad, the men will be arriving tomorrow morning."

"The men? What men?"

"The men to dig our cave."

I set my cup down hard on the saucer. "Our *cave*?"

"Yes, They will dig into that slope at the end of the yard." He pointed one long finger and I turned to look. "It is quite high enough."

"High enough for what? I don't understand. What are we to do with a cave?"

"Sleep in it, and possibly live in it."

"Derek! I find that a most unpleasant idea! A *cave*?"

"Don't fret, Tad." He reached over and patted my arm. "It will be quite comfortable. I just wanted you to know they were coming to start the work."

In case anyone ever reads this jumbled record I am keeping, I suppose I should admit to a certain weakness I have always had. It is something I am ashamed of but cannot overcome, and it is caused by what I think of as "earthy" things. The most innocent earthworms, wriggling into their holes, fat spiders in their sticky webs, and other harmless creatures such as these fill me with aversion. But worst of all is being underground. Years ago our parents often took us to visit ancient churches, and we would go down to the undercrofts below. I can still feel the choking panic, the chill sweat that used to break out on my body, the rapid beating of my heart. Yet I never admitted it to Mamma nor Papa, and certainly never to Derek. As soon as we reached ground level again I would recover quickly and not think of it until whenever the next time might be. Now, the very thought of a *cave* ... if I could only have wished it away!

But the men arrived as promised, early the following morning. Two sturdy black men appeared, riding in a small cart, pulled by a lethargic donkey. In the cart were their shovels, several thick wooden posts and boards, and a collection of odds and ends that indicated they could handle almost any sort of handyman job. I went outdoors to speak to them, and after looking our small yard over carefully they found a spot they considered suitable.

"Right in here, missy," one said. "This is the best place."

I tried to make my voice light. "It seems so silly to hide in a cave."

The man looked solemn. "Better to hide in a cave and come out of it alive, than to hide in a house and have the roof crash in."

I was not certain I agreed. In any case, they worked every day for a week, and as they advanced deeper into the earth they shored it up with the wooden posts, and laid the boards as flooring. When the cave was completed it had a shelf to hold a lamp or water or other small supplies and was quite large enough for several people. One could easily stand upright in it. As caves go I suppose it was satisfactory. Others were being dug deep into the firm Vicksburg clay, some quite large with separate rooms, ceilings, storage cupboards, and other conveniences. The thought of spending any time inside one made the dampness start out on my forehead.

Betsy loved the place. She sat inside for hours playing with a rag doll she was fond of, humming happily to herself, and talking to Woof, who must have found it cool and pleasant. Better they than I, I thought.

Mid-May 1862

BY THE MIDDLE OF MAY 1862, THE BLOCKADE PINCH was impossible to ignore. All my life I had taken for granted the fact that there would always be food on the table, tea to drink, spices and flour and butter and sugar to cook with. Since I had lived with Derry I had enjoyed planning meals and shopping, choosing foods we both liked, debating with Amanda whether to select ham or lamb, chicken or fish, beef or veal. But all that had changed.

Part of the Western Flotilla (so carefully explained to me by Ben) lurked in the river just south of us, with a man named Phillips Lee in command. In the two hundred miles that separate Vicksburg from Memphis, other Union boats were gathered, apparently slipping through the Confederate batteries at night. No Southern shipping could get by them. The blockade was total.

Those townspeople who had plantations east of Vicksburg could still reach them. They brought back whatever vegetables or fruit were available, and for the most part were very generous with their friends. The Blairs gave us beans and potatoes and carrots and onions, and occasionally peaches or plums or a fowl. But the shops were almost empty, not only of food, but of virtually everything.

I had wanted some straight pins to use while mend-ing a shirt of Derek's, but there were none in any shop. I took to picking up any pin I found, straightening it, cleaning it of rust, and putting it carefully away. All this for a pin!

Mary Byrd came calling one afternoon, limping into the house with one shabby slipper in her hand.

"What on earth . . ." I began.

She held it up, a rueful smile on her pretty face. "Most of the top is behind me somewhere in the street. It simply came apart from the sole. And there is not a pair of shoes in Vicksburg! I know. I have been trying for a week to find new ones."

I took the shoe from her and looked at it carefully. "We might be able to remake it, Mary Byrd. We could try."

Her expression was skeptical to say the very least. "There were no classes in shoemaking when I went to school," she said.

"No, but neither was there a war. We are going to have to use our wits for a lot of things, I think." I opened a chest we had brought with us from England, in which were packed clothes that were far too warm for the Mississippi climate. Searching through them I found a heavy dark blue coat I had worn during London winters, and held it up.

"Would you care for blue, madam?" I asked, as if I were a shopkeeper.

Mary Byrd's eyes sparkled. "Do you really think we can, Rosemary?"

"There is but one way to be sure," I told her solemnly.

We fetched strong scissors and carefully removed the fragile shredded leather from the sole of the slipper. Using that as a sort of pattern, I cut two new tops. With a needle and heavy thread I sewed the thick fabric to the soles, pricking my finger repeatedly and fussing under my breath. Mary Byrd watched with flattering admiration.

"Rosemary, I do believe you are a genius! I should never have thought of that."

"Oh yes, you would have. It's what my mother would have called 'making do,' and I fancy we are both going to have to 'make do' in many ways."

It took an hour or more to complete the slippers, but we were both inordinately pleased with the result. Mary Byrd slipped them on her feet and minced about the room.

"I declare they are more comfortable than the old ones! From now on I shall wear nothing on my feet except shoes made from old coats!" She laughed and hugged me. "What an extraordinary person you are, honey," she said, and then her face grew serious. "And you're right about 'making do.' I think we had best not throw one blessed thing away. Heaven only knows when life will be the way it used to be—maybe never. So I guess we better be mighty smart about keeping, and saving—and 'making do.' "

I laughed. I couldn't help it. The idea of my butterfly friend being so practical was comical. After a moment she laughed with me.

"I know," she said. "You think I'm nothing but a silly girl who likes parties and dancing and pretty clothes and having a good time. And you're almost right. But I'm a Southern girl, Rosemary, and we're tougher than you think. Whatever has to be done to get us through this war, I can do."

I took her hand and pressed it. "I know you can, Mary Byrd."

And again her smile flashed. "And if I *can't*, then I'll just come to you. Between us, we can do anything!"

And she left, the new slippers on her feet. It was strange to realize Mary Byrd was almost two years older than I. She seemed such a dainty, charming, pleasure-loving child. I could not imagine her enduring any sort of hardship.

It was about that time that Derry announced one evening we were going to sleep in the cave.

"But Derry, *why*? There is no danger."

"I agree that at the moment there is none, Tad, but some night those boats that are down the river—and the boats that are up the river—are going to converge on Vicksburg. It will not be pleasant. We may well spend not only nights but also days in that cave, and we should become accustomed to it. See if there are any small changes we want to make. So we are going to sleep there tonight."

Derek's opinion of me has always been, and still is, important. I simply could not bring myself to tell him how much I loathed the notion of even entering that dank cave, let alone sleeping in it. To use one of our childhood expressions, he would think I was cracked! And perhaps I was.

Derry tried to lighten my silence. "I suppose you'd rather live in that tamarack tree, wouldn't you?" he asked.

I managed a small laugh. "At least I can't fall out of the cave and bloody my knee, can I?" I said, and felt rather proud of myself.

So that night we undressed in the house, gathered up blankets and pillows, took a surprised but joyful Woof with us, and walked across our small backyard to the cave. Derry had hung a sheet as a curtain to divide the space, and had laid mattresses on the board floor. He had supplied us each with a candle in a holder, and there was a covered jar of water on the shelf.

"Our cozy little home," I muttered, trying to keep my teeth from chattering.

"Yes. Romantic, isn't it?"

"An earthworm might find it so."

But there was nothing to do except lie down and make myself as comfortable as I could. Woof prowled a bit as if wondering what his beloved humans were doing in a place he had considered his and Betsy's domain, then settled himself down in the entranceway with a thump and a few grunts.

I lay so that I could look through the cave opening and see the stars. That helped. I did not feel so shut in, so trapped. The place was damp, with a clayey smell that I found disturbing, but it was not as terrifying as I had feared it would be. With my eyes on the faint stars I wondered who would have thought that a well-brought-up young lady like Rosemary Monica Stafford Leigh and her handsome, brilliant brother would come to this. A snug, dry little house, and they prefer to huddle in a yellow clay cave dug into the side of a hill! Suddenly it seemed very funny. I tried to stifle a giggle, but it was useless. The giggle grew into a chuckle, and then into a gale of laughter. Derry's head poked round the curtain.

"What in the name of ..."

I couldn't stop. I tried to speak and the words were lost in spasms of laughter. Then somehow the laughter was mixed with tears and I didn't know whether I was laughing or crying. I felt myself pulled to a sitting position and Derek's hand, filled with cold water from the jar, slapped into my face.

"Stop it, Tad! You're hysterical!"

I gasped and looked up at him, his face barely visible in the faint starlight.

"Sorry," I hiccuped.

"Are you all right now?"

"I think so."

"Then try to go to sleep. Do you want to hold my hand under the curtain?"

"No. I'll be all right."

He knelt there a moment, looking at me. Then he gently dried my face with a corner of the blanket and patted my cheek.

"Go to sleep, my little cavewoman. Good night."

"Good night, Derry. And—I'm sorry."

"Don't worry."

Surprisingly I fell asleep almost at once. When I awoke the first early sunrays were slanting into my face.

May 18, 1862

SOMETIMES WAITING FOR SOMETHING BAD TO HAPPEN is worse than the actuality. Each morning when I awoke I would run to the windows and scan the river far below. Since a great stretch of it had been cleared of all Southern craft, any boat I saw, I reasoned, was a Union boat. They would hover silently out there on the water, well away from the Vicksburg side, watching us, memorizing our coastline, making no move to fire. Sometimes Confederate sharpshooters, concealed by shrubbery or perched high in trees, would be close enough to pick off a few hapless crew members while escaping any injury to themselves, but everyone knew that a moment would come when the great flotilla would spring into action, and it was harrowing to think that the very next minute might be the one.

In the meantime we tried to go about our business, which is just what I was doing one afternoon when I chanced to walk by a window and, looking out, saw flames leaping high near the riverside. My heart almost stopped! We're being fired on by the ships, I thought. The moment has come!

It was time for Derek to come home, and as I watched anxiously for him I thought of the abandoned warehouses that stood by the river. Uncle Will's office was not far above those buildings. If sparks flew, where might they not land? By the time I finally saw Hector—not Derry—I was frantic. I rushed to meet him.

"Hector! Where's Mr. Derek? I can see flames down there—where is he? Are they firing from the ships? Was it a shell?"

"Whoa, Miss Rosemary! Stop your fretting. Your brother is all right. *All* right." The enormous man stepped in and closed the door. "Some old crates right nearby caught fire and the river wind blew some little old bits of burning wood up against a corner of the office, right where Mr. Stafford keeps his law papers and records and the like. . . ."

"Is he hurt, Hector? Is Derek hurt?"

Amanda and Betsy had come into the room quietly, as Hector was speaking. Now Betsy went to her father, putting her arm around one of his sturdy legs, thrusting the comforting thumb into her mouth.

"Miss Rosemary, I promise you they are both all right. Do you think I'd have left them in bad trouble? Now don't you fret."

"It's all very well to tell people not to fret," I said peevishly, "but maybe the whole office will go up in smoke and . . ."

Amanda gave my shoulder a gentle shake. "Now Miss Rosemary, don't carry on. Those are two grown men with sense. Nothing's going to happen to them. If Hector says they're all right, they are."

Half ashamed, I looked at her. Amanda and Hector both stood so tall and straight, they seemed so strong, so quiet, not like the many Negroes who shambled along the streets, talking in loud, shrill voices. Even their speech had little trace of dialect.

"Where did you both learn to speak so well?" The question just popped out of my mouth. And then I blushed! What an impertinent thing to say! I tried to apologize. "I'm sorry—I never should have . . ."

Amanda laughed. I had never heard her really laugh before. "You're feeling a little better now, aren't you? Good! Let's make ourselves comfortable somewhere, and get to know each other."

"In the cave," Betsy chirped. "Let's all sit in the cave and Dada will tell us stories."

"The cave?" I couldn't imagine a less inviting place to sit.

"Yes. It's nice and cool, and Woof likes it. Let's all go." Betsy tugged at her father's hand. "Come along, Dada."

I turned back to a smiling Hector. "Are you positively *sure* Derek and Uncle Will are all right?" I asked.

"Miss Rosemary, if those two men were in any trouble I'd be right there with them. I told you that."

"I know you did, and I know it's true. It's just that I worry . . ."

"Of course you do. But this time there's no need. You believe me?"

"I believe you, Hector."

"Fine, Miss Romy," Betsy said. "If everybody believes everybody is all right, then we can sit in the cave and tell stories. I'll find Woof." And she trotted from the room, calling her furry friend.

I went with them to the door and then outside and

around the little house and into the cave. I settled onto
my mattress, pulling my legs up under my skirts, with
Amanda on one side of me and Hector, with Betsy
comfortably perched on his lap, on the other. Woof col-
lapsed at my feet with a deep, contented sigh. I turned
to Amanda.

"I'm sorry I was so inquisitive," I said. "But you
both speak so beautifully—not at all like .... like the
other people I hear on the street."

"It's nice to have you say that. My teacher would be
pleased. He worked very hard!" She smiled as she
spoke.

"Who was he?" I asked.

"He was a white preacher who came from the North
to a little church quite a way from here. When he
wasn't preaching he taught school in the church building. There were eight, ten of us youngsters, and we all
thought Preacher Thomas was about the greatest man
we'd ever known. We tried so hard to be like him, to
talk as he did, to do everything he wanted—it was
probably the easiest teaching he ever did. We learned
to read with him, mostly from the Bible, and to figure.
He had maps, and he tried to teach us something about
the world. I remember how hard it was to believe there
was so much world we knew nothing about. I went to
that little school for close to six years before he moved
away. I never went to school again."

I took her hand in mine. "He must have been a wonderful teacher."

From her seat on Hector's lap Betsy piped up.

"Dada went to school in 'Beria. Didn't you, Dada?"

"Liberia, Betsy. *Li*beria."

"*Li*beria. In Africa. Tell us about when you were a little boy and lived there. And tell about the prince."

"Seems like I should be doing something more useful than spinning yarns," Hector said, but his voice had that rumbling chuckle in it.

"Yarns are very useful," Betsy said firmly. "They get Miss Romy to stop fretting. So tell!"

"Yes, Hector," I added. "Please tell. A real prince?"

"As real as they come, Miss Rosemary. But the prince comes later. You know what 'Liberia' means? It means Place of Freedom. That's what the American Colonization Society called it when they started it about 1822. That was two years after I was born there. My parents were farming folk—they had a good spread of land and we lived right well. They wanted me to have more book learning than they'd ever had, and when I was big enough they sent me to a little school in the nearest village. Didn't have a Preacher Thomas," Hector grinned at his wife, "but there were good-hearted women from that society who took us in hand."

"But exactly what did this Colonization Society do?" I asked.

"They made it a country where they could send slaves to become free people. Most everybody there had been slaves here in the South, or they were the children of slaves, and nearly every slave is an African. Africa is where slaves come from."

"And were your parents slaves?"

"Never! They both came from farm people and they were as free as any person ever is."

"Then why did you come to America?"

"That's going to be a long story, Miss Rosemary."

"Please tell it. And where does this prince come into it?"

Hector arranged Betsy more comfortably on his lap and leaned his great shoulders against the wall of the cave. "I first heard about the prince from his grandson, Simon. Simon and I, we were the same age, and we both went to the society ladies' school. He had been just a baby when he and his mama and his daddy were bought free from the man who owned them—a Mr. Foster, he was—and sent to Liberia. The society liked to keep families all together when they could, and sometimes they could buy a whole family and free them. So, Simon and I, we grew up together and he used to spend long hours telling me about his grand-daddy, Prince." A half-sad smile was on Hector's face, and his eyes looked way back in time. "Prince!" he repeated.

Betsy jiggled his arm. "Don't just keep saying 'Prince,' tell the story, Dada!"

"Well," Hector went on, "Prince was the son of a king, King Sori of the Fulbe empire. His true name was Abd al-Rahman Ibrahim, but that was hard to get my tongue around and I just always called him Prince. He was born in Timbuktu in Africa, some ways from Liberia. He grew up to be a brave soldier, and a tall, handsome man.

"All African people lived in tribes, and, like everywhere, there was war between the tribes. One tribe might have cattle another tribe wanted, or good pastureland, or a man from one tribe might fancy himself a special woman from another, and so there were battles. When the winning tribe took captives they made them into slaves. Then—sometime—they heard how big planters in America wanted to buy slaves to work on their plantations. The winning tribes liked this. They got rid of their captives and got money for them, too. So there was a great stream of African folks loaded onto boats and brought here. They were chained together and marched many miles to a seaport, and then they were sold and shipped away."

I was aghast. "You mean—Africans *sold* Africans? Into slavery?"

Hector gazed straight at me and his face was tight. "You think black men are better than others?" His voice was bitter. "There are mean men and there are good men, and the color of their skin doesn't change what's inside. Don't ever forget that, Miss Rosemary."

"I won't," I whispered.

"Well, that's what happened to Prince. He was captured in a big battle and he was sold. He tried to tell everybody he was a royal man and his daddy, the king, would pay good money for him, but nobody listened. He was put on a ship to Natchez. A lot of the captives died on those ships. They were in chains the whole time, they were fed spoiled food and didn't have enough water, and they couldn't stand up because the place they were kept—the hold, it's called—was too low. But Prince was strong, and he lived, and when they landed he was sold right off to that Mr. Foster. The prince was twenty-six years old then. What a well-favored man he must have been!"

Hector stopped. There was anguish in his eyes. I did not want to speak. After a moment he went on.

"Well," he said, taking a deep breath, "Prince was strong and quiet and sort of—a leader. He told Mr. Foster that he had had schooling, and that his daddy would pay to get him back, but Mr. Foster figured he had got himself a special slave and he kept him. He found a wife for Prince—even though Prince told him he had a wife in Africa, and a little son, too.

"Mr Foster was passable kind to his slaves, didn't beat them near as much as some. Prince was so good with the other slaves Mr. Foster made him a foreman. And the plantation grew, and the best cotton was raised and sold and the best prices paid, and it was all because of Prince. And a lot of years went by. All this Simon told me, when we were boys."

"Did you ever see him? Prince?"

"Yes, I saw him. I was nine years old. He got his freedom at last and came to Liberia."

"Oh, how wonderful!" I suddenly felt relieved. "And then he went back to his family? And his father, the king?"

"No, Miss Rosemary. Not as easy as that. He was a slave for fifty years before he found a white man who helped him get free. Fifty years! Prince was an old man when he came back. He died just a little time after he got there. He was an old man, but he still stood straight and tall. He still had a nose like a hawk, but his hair had gone all white. I'll never forget him!"

"Fifty years," I repeated. "Oh, Hector, how can there be slavery?"

"It's just natural, I reckon. Everybody wants to be a big man, have somebody else to do his work for him. And if they've got the money they can do just that."

There was silence for a moment and I tried to encompass the idea of a world where slavery was a natural condition. Amanda got to her feet, giving my shoulder a little pat as she rose.

"I better start us some dinner. Mr. Derek will be home soon."

Hector stood up, putting a drowsy Betsy on her feet. He put out a hand to help me up. It was strong and warm on mine. I looked up at him.

"Thank you, Hector."

He smiled. "For what, Miss Rosemary? For spinning yarns?"

"For helping me understand things I know so little about."

We stepped out into the early evening, and I could hear the gentle sound of birds and wagon wheels and faraway voices. As we walked toward the house I said, "But you didn't tell us how you came to America. Nor why."

"We'll save that for another time. Look. I think that's Mr. Derek coming up the hill."

It was. I ran to meet him and we went indoors together.

May 22-27, 1862

ON A THURSDAY EVENING LATE IN MAY DEREK AND I
watched from our windows as a forest of masts glided
ghostlike up the river toward us. Phillips Lee's flotilla.
A great hush seemed to have fallen over the waiting
city. It was so silent I wanted to scream, yet I found
myself whispering.

"Why doesn't someone shoot?"

"Too dark. It would be wasted. The boats are still beyond our range."

"But are we beyond *their* range?"

"They are just not ready yet, Tad. They're going to
keep us waiting. It's a cat-and-mouse game."

And keep us waiting they did. All the next day
passed without a single shot. Saturday dragged by,
and Sunday. We heard many theories. "Old Yanks are
sizing up the situation and finding out there's not a
thing they can do." And, "They see they can shoot at
us all they want, but if they try to land we'll get 'em
one by one."

And Monday morning came, clear and bright, and
still there was nothing. The whole affair became a little
ridiculous, and I lost interest in staring down at the
river.

It was precisely five o'clock that Monday afternoon,
May 26, when I went into the kitchen, as was my habit,
to see what Amanda had scraped together for our sup-

per. I looked down at the inevitable cornmeal, some dried beans, some bits of chicken left from last night's meal—it was one the Blairs had given us—and a jar of tomatoes, put up by Amanda the summer before when crops were plentiful.

I recall saying to her, "What on earth can you do with these things?" and Amanda replying, "I'll make a sort of gumbo, Miss Rosemary. You'll find it tasty," and then we heard a muffled boom.

We both ran into the little parlor and peered out of the window, trying to get a clear view between the trees. A dot of white smoke hung over the river. That was all we could see.

"You think this is it, Miss Rosemary?" Amanda asked, her eyes wide.

"I don't know. There was just one shot—maybe it came from our batteries."

"No, it came from one of those ships. That smoke was over the river, and the smoke comes when they fire the guns. Hector told me that."

The front door opened and Derry came in from work. "Can you see anything?" he asked by way of greeting.

"Not much. Just a puff of white smoke over the river."

But as we watched we counted twenty shots from the ships. They made a different, heavier sound than that of the fire returned by the defending troops. After a while the masts retreated down the river and silence returned.

The next day, Tuesday, May 27, passed quietly and I

decided to take Woof for a walk in the afternoon. I was able to buy four eggs from a neighbor who still kept a few chickens, and started home. As I neared our house, the line of ships moved slowly into sight. I was too far away to hear the steam-driven engines, and the hush made the silent procession of power eerie and frightening. I stood in front of our house, squinting against the sunlight that glinted on the brasswork of the boats, and saw that first puff of smoke from the leading vessel before I heard the dull, echoing report. Shells were fired in rapid succession, and after a stunned moment I ran into the house.

"So they're back," Amanda said flatly.

"They're back," I replied, and carefully handed her the eggs.

By the time Derry came home the firing had been going on for an hour or more, but it all seemed to come from the ships, not from the city's fortifications. I asked him why.

"We'd be wasting ammunition," he explained. "The Union ships stay as far out in the river as they can. They aren't easy to reach. We learned that yesterday. Vicksburg's ammunition is limited, Tad, like everything else. It would be foolish to waste it."

When we sat down to supper the firing had stopped, and I breathed in the stillness gratefully.

"Maybe it's all over," I said. "Maybe the ships have found it is useless to . . ."

"It hasn't even begun, Tad. It hasn't even begun."

It was still quiet when Amanda and Betsy left to go

home to Hector. Derek sat reading *The Citizen*, which got smaller day by day as the supply of paper diminished, and I sat across from him, trying valiantly to knit my first pair of "patriotic" socks. He looked at me over the paper, one eyebrow raised.

"What in the world are you doing, Tad?"

"Trying to knit a sock. Mary Byrd gave me a skein of wool and said I should try."

"For some lucky boy in gray?"

"I doubt it will ever be for anyone. But if I don't do something with my hands they keep shaking."

Derry gave me a long look, his eyes serious. Then he said, "It sometimes occurs to me that I have a rather wonderful little sister." He turned his gaze back to *The Citizen*. I felt warm inside.

When the next barrage of shells went off I dropped those uneven rows of knitting on the floor, the needles slipping from the wool. Derek rose, laying the paper aside.

"Come along, Tad. It's the cave tonight."

I didn't argue. Woof took up his post at the door of the cave, Derry and I bedded down, and after I had said my prayer—the simple one Mamma had taught me years ago—I lay there listening to the constant whine of the shells. When I heard the crunching thud and felt the vibration, I thrust my hand under the dividing sheet to find Derry's. It was right there.

"I think that one hit something," I said.

"I think you're right."

It was impossible to sleep. Finally we dragged a mattress near the cave entrance and huddled there. We could see flames from farther down the hill and the shelling continued. Woof trembled and I smoothed him, though it didn't calm either one of us. He nuzzled his cold nose into my hand and whimpered.

Suddenly my brother threw himself across me, pushing me half off the mattress. As my chin scraped on the board floor I heard a terrifying whine and then a dreadful solid thump, accompanied by a rending, cracking, splintering sound. From under Derry's body I managed to say, "Our house?"

"Our house. Move way back in the cave, Tad. I'll go and see."

"Oh no, you won't!" I grabbed his arm and held tightly. "You are not moving out of this place until the firing stops!"

Derry looked at me through the dimness. "All right," he said. "We'll wait. At least it wasn't an incendiary. We would see flames by now."

And so we sat for the rest of that interminable night, leaning against the back wall, knees drawn up and covered with a blanket.

The shelling stopped about three in the morning.

May 28, 1862

MORNING

THE MOON WAS STILL VISIBLE WHEN WE CREPT OUT OF the cave in the predawn light and walked around the tiny yard, looking up at our house. At first I could see no damage, and my heart rose.

"The roof," Derek said, pointing upwards. I *wish* he could not always read my thoughts so well! As my eyes followed his hand I could see the sickeningly large hole, directly over his room.

"Wait here, Tad. I'll go in and take a look."

"It's my house as much as yours, and I am not about to stand out here in my nightclothes. I'm coming in with you."

"Very well, my modest maiden, but let me go first."

He opened the backdoor and entered, Woof and I close behind him. We walked through the kitchen and the tiny dining room. "So far, so good," my brother said.

It didn't last. In the middle of the parlor floor lay a large fragment of a shell, surrounded by plaster and white dust.

"Is it going to explode?"

"No, Tad. It has done everything it was meant to do."

I looked up. One leg of Derry's bed was hanging through a hole in the ceiling. Treading carefully, Derek walked around the mess on the floor and started up the stairs, and I was right behind him. Woof paused to investigate the shell, sniffing warily and sneezing.

The door to Derek's room stood open, and the room was littered with chunks of plaster, pieces of wood, and bits of shattered shingles from the roof. His shaving mirror had fallen from his dresser and lay broken on the floor, mixed with bits of glass from a window. Apparently a piece of the shell had gone through the wall between our rooms, and I turned to look into my own chamber. There were plaster and wood chips and white dust everywhere, but the furniture seemed intact.

"It's not so bad, Derry, is it? Amanda and I will clean up all this plaster mess, and then we can have the roof mended, and we'll be all right."

"The roof, and the floor, and the parlor ceiling, and the wall between our rooms. And where, in this blockaded city, are we to find wood for new rafters, and shingles for the roof, and more wood for this floor, and plaster—to say nothing of workmen? I'll try, Tad, but I suspect we won't be living here any longer."

"Then where?"

He didn't answer directly. "Get dressed, and stay away from broken places lest more loosened plaster comes down. The kitchen seems safe enough and a little breakfast might be welcome. I'll see you there presently."

I dressed obediently, shaking plaster dust off everything I touched. As I was going down the stairs I heard a great knocking on our front door, and then the sound of the door opening. As I reached the bottom I walked straight into Ben Fraser, wide-eyed and white-faced.

"Are you all right?" he asked.

"Our house was hit."

"I noticed. Are you in one piece? Where's Derek?"

"Dressing. We slept in the cave last night. At least, we didn't precisely *sleep* . . ."

"I am sure not. I was just riding by, and I saw. Thank God you're not hurt, Rosemary! When I saw the house—are you sure-to-God you're not hurt anywhere?" He took my arm, shaking it gently. "Oh, Rosemary, if anything had happened to you . . ."

I was surprised and a bit embarrassed at his distress. "I'm quite all right, Ben. Come into the kitchen while I get breakfast."

While Ben built up a fire in the range I fetched a loaf of cornmeal bread Amanda had made, decided recklessly to use the little coffee that remained in the canister, and found a jar of peach preserves put up the summer before. It looked like a sparse meal, so I threw caution to the winds and added a jar of figs. As I was filling Woof's water dish, Derry came into the kitchen.

"Good morning, Ben. What brings you out so early?"

"I go on duty at six. It must be close to that now. I was passing and saw the house. Are you sure you are both unhurt?"

"Absolutely. Sit down and have breakfast with us. Will you be court-martialed if you're late?"

"I doubt if my absence would be noticed. We've all been busy ducking the Yankee shells."

As so often happens, food had a very beneficial effect. Ben removed the piece of shell from the parlor floor, asked several times more whether both Derek and I were unhurt, and finally departed. I fetched a broom and started sweeping up the rest of the debris, and Derry prepared to leave for the office. Just before he opened the door he turned to me.

"Promise me something, Tad."

"What?"

"If shelling should start again, take Amanda and Betsy and Woof and go into the cave. Promise."

"I will. I promise." Somehow the cave didn't seem as hateful this morning. "What about our house, Derry? About fixing it?"

"I'll talk to Uncle Will. We'll think of something. Remember now, if there is any ..."

"I know. I promised. Don't worry, Derry."

And I stood in the doorway and waved to him as he started down the street.

When Amanda arrived I was in my bedroom, trying to clean the plastery, powdery mess. She came up the stairs and stopped in the little hall, looking into both chambers. She spoke quietly.

"You all right, Miss Rosemary?"

"Yes, Amanda. Derek and I slept in the cave last night. We were there when it happened. We heard it."

Unexpectedly all the tension and fright rose to the surface and my eyes filled with tears. Amanda looked at me and said the wrong thing.

"You poor child! Just getting settled in a new land

under your own roof and the Yankees come along and blow it off!"

It was too much! I sank in a heap on my bed and the tears came in earnest. "My dear little house," I sobbed. "I love it so much, and now . . . oooohh!" And I fell face down, crying like a baby.

I felt the bed move as Amanda sat down beside me, and then I was gathered into warm arms and held tight, while her soft voice crooned to me.

"There, child, there. Cry it all out now. It will make you feel better."

She was right. It did. After a few minutes I sat up, Amanda washed my face with cool water as if I were a baby indeed, and presently we tied on our aprons and set to work cleaning as much of the residue as we could. When we were through I had to wash my hair. It was white from plaster dust.

It wasn't long before Mary Byrd came racing in, and again I had to repeat over and over that neither Derek nor I was hurt.

"How did you know about it?" I asked.

"Cousin Benjamin told us. He came riding hell-for-leather and at first I could hardly make head nor tail of the story because it was filled with 'sure-to-God scared' and 'great holes in the roof' and your name about twenty times, sugar, and he just went on and on, but at last we got the story out of him and so I came as fast as I could. Oh, Rosemary, thank the Lord you are both all right!"

"Amen," I said.

May 28, 1862

MARY BYRD WAS STILL THERE WHEN DEREK CAME home, and I saw her eyes race over him from head to toe, checking for damage. She had to hear the whole tale again from Derry. He said some very complimentary things about my behavior, which made me glad he had not been at home when I went all to pieces in Amanda's arms.

"What are you going to do now?" Mary Byrd asked. "Are men coming to repair the roof?"

"No," Derek said flatly. "The best they could do would be to cover the hole with canvas, which hardly seems secure enough. No, I have found us another house. Or, to be totally honest, Uncle Will found it."

"Where?" I asked.

He told us the name of the street, which I did not recognize, but Mary Byrd did.

"Way up there?" she said. "Seems like those are pretty fancy houses way up there. Pretty fancy and pretty big."

"Correct on both counts. This house is pretty fancy, and it is also pretty big. *And,* most important of all, it is the only house available in the city. It belongs to a family named Bartlett who removed themselves to a safer area and will not return until this is all over."

Mary Byrd's blue eyes stretched wide. "Bartlett?"

she repeated. "Mr. and Mrs. George Bartlett?" Derry nodded. "Why, we know them! One of the finest families in Vicksburg." Then she broke into peals of laughter. "Oh, I do declare! The idea of you two living in that ..."

"What's the matter with it, Mary Byrd?" I demanded. "Why is it so comical? What is wrong with the house?"

"It's a mansion, is what it is. It makes our house look real puny. You'll be rattling around like dried peas in a hopper." She laughed delightedly, her words bubbling through. "It will take you an hour to walk all through the house, and you'll need a map. You had best train Woof to find you if you get lost." Trying to control her laughter, she turned to Derek. "When are you going to move?"

"Now," he said. "Right now. Hector has brought a wagon and we are moving out right now. Tomorrow he will tack canvas over the roof to keep out the rain."

"The Bartlett house!" Mary Byrd giggled again. She has a most contagious giggle. It made me want to laugh with her. "I do declare!" She picked up a basket she had brought and held it out to me. It looked very much like the one Woof had first arrived in and I stared at her suspiciously.

"*Not* another puppy," I said.

Mary Byrd laughed again. "No, sugar, this is a picnic supper for you to have tonight. Mama always feeds people when trouble hits them. I'll help, too. I just have to be there when your eyes pop out!"

Derry's dark eyebrows lifted whimsically. "We certainly don't want to deny you any little pleasures, Mary Byrd, and we'll be glad of your help. You two girls go to work on Tad's things."

Mary Byrd's eyes seemed to caress my brother's face. "Whatever you say, Derek," she murmured demurely.

There was something unusual about her tone. This was not the flirtatious butterfly I had often watched in her dealings with young men: she seemed content to do whatever Derry asked. I glanced quickly at him to see what his reaction might be. Save that his eyes lingered on hers for a moment I could tell nothing.

I led the way upstairs to my room where we began laying clothing in wicker trunks. Mary Byrd chattered away as she generally did and in the midst of it I heard the front door open and close. Looking down the stairs I saw Ben Fraser's tawny thatch.

"Hello," I called.

He looked up. "Hello there. You're moving?"

"Yes. Into Buckingham Palace, I gather. Derry will tell you."

"I've come to help."

"How nice! Don't soldiers ever have to be on duty?"

"Occasionally. Anyhow, one of our duties is taking care of the citizens of Vicksburg." He pulled off his uniform jacket. "Now, friend Leigh, where shall I start?"

With Amanda and Betsy clearing the kitchen of all that belonged to us, and Mary Byrd and me packing clothes and personal items, and Ben and Derek loading books and bedding and the small pieces of furniture that were ours, and Hector stowing things in the large

wagon and in the buggy Mary Byrd had arrived in,
and Woof bouncing from one person to another in a
frenzy of excitement, it did not take us long. We filed
out of our little house, and I looked back just as Derry
was turning the key in the lock. I could feel a lump of
tears rising in my throat, and then Mary Byrd caught
my arm.

"This way, sugar. You and I will ride in my buggy,
and Ben will be our outrider, and Woof can protect
us on the other side, and the rest of them can go in
the wagon. Now, just you hoist yourself up into the
seat . . ." She bustled about, patting Ben's horse on the
rump to move him out of the way, hustling me into the
buggy seat, hopping lightly up beside me, calling
orders to Woof, shaking the reins and clucking to her
horse, and before I could look back again at the house I
had loved so dearly, we were well away from it. Blessings on her!

We must have made an odd procession as we went
higher and higher up the steep streets until I feared we
would surely topple down. Ben rode beside us, Woof
trotted obediently on the other side, and Mary Byrd
chattered on until I felt my voice was steady enough to
join in. At last we turned into a drive that curved
across a broad lawn set with flowering shrubs and tall
old trees. Ahead of us the house glowed in the late afternoon sun, and I gasped with astonishment.

"Good heavens, Mary Byrd, it *is* a mansion!"

"I told you so," she said, gloating.

Of deep red brick, it stood three stories high, with
lacy white iron galleries across all three floors. On each

level there was a wide center door, flanked by tall windows framed by gleaming white shutters. From the front veranda to the molded eaves, six white wooden columns marched across the house, their bases and tops beautifully carved. It was an elegant house, and rather awesome.

Derry jumped down from the wagon and walked back to me. "Well, there it is. The only house available. What do you say?"

"What *can* I say? But it's so enormous!"

"It is a trifle roomy. But I suggest we use only the first floor. Even that will be more than adequate. Come in and look."

Taking a large key from his pocket Derry opened the wide front door and stood aside while we all entered. Mary Byrd's eyes sparkled as she watched me.

"Wasn't I right?" she asked gleefully.

"You were right!"

Stunned, I wandered from one room to another. Furnishings were sparse, the Bartletts must have taken many items with them. We went from the vast entrance hall through a parlor, a music room, a study, a dining room large enough to hold a banquet, a library, a butler's pantry, various storage pantries, and finally, a great kitchen. I was speechless.

"I suggest you use the music room as your bedroom, Tad," Derek said. "If you can't sleep you can always play the harp. I'll take the study. We'll close off the dining room and parlor lest we get lost, and take our meals in the library."

"I shall feel like Queen Victoria roaming around Windsor Castle. I'm sure this is larger than Buckingham Palace, but if it is our only choice—then let's move in!"

We unloaded the wagon and the buggy. The picnic basket was delivered to Amanda, and Hector and Ben and Derry brought two bedsteads downstairs. As Hector and Derry worked on my bed I heard Hector say quietly, "Seems sort of strange that it's *this* house, doesn't it, Mr. Derek?"

My brother gave him a quick glance. "Yes, it does. But it can't make any difference now. Those times are over, I hope."

"Pray God you are right, sir," Hector said softly, and that was all.

I wondered what they were talking about, and then forgot it as Mary Byrd and I spread the beds neatly with our linen and blankets. It seemed to me she gave an extra little pat to the pillow she placed on Derek's bed. Just as we finished Betsy came racing in.

"Mama says you-all come out on the lawn for supper. It's going to be a picnic, Miss Romy!"

"What fun," I said. "We'll come right away."

Tired but exhilarated, we went outdoors to find a blanket spread on the grass. On the veranda Amanda had laid out the most delectable and astonishing meal I had seen in months! Hard-cooked eggs, most likely from our former generous neighbor, small slices of pink ham—

"Mary Byrd! Where did the ham come from?"

"I reckon Mamma put it in the basket. We still have one or two in the smokehouse."

Bowls of preserves, bread (cornmeal bread, of course, but so thinly sliced it looked delicious), a bowl of fresh plums—"Plums?"

"There's a plum tree way out back," Amanda said with satisfaction. "Betsy found it, and I boosted her up to fetch us a few."

It was a feast! As we settled ourselves on the blanket, Hector came round the side of the house, smiling widely, a dusty bottle held high in each hand.

"To toast the new house," he announced.

Derek tried to sound stern. "Hector! Where did you find those?"

The big man shrugged in innocence. "I was just looking round the cellar, Mr. Derek, and I saw all these bottles. Figure nobody's going to miss two."

"The cellar, hmm?"

"Yes, sir. That cellar."

Derry shook his head, but he was smiling. "Very well, a toast to the new house."

It was impossible to think we were in a city at war, and so we did not. We toasted everything we could think of, we laughed, we ate. At last Derry and I walked with Mary Byrd and Ben to the buggy and horses.

"Thank you both," I said, "so very, very much! I don't know how we should have managed without you."

"Live happy here," Mary Byrd said, and held out her hand to Derek.

My brother took it, his eyes on hers, and gently laid his other hand on her cheek. I could see her flush. "Our dear friend," was all he said.

He helped her into the buggy, Ben mounted his horse, and Derek and I stood waving as they started down the long drive. The sun had gone, and deep twilight cast soft shadows over everything. We turned and stood looking up at the house.

"We'll call it the Tamarack Tree, Tad," Derry said. "It's just about as high as you can get."

June 1862

In June the city of Memphis, Tennessee, was taken after a naval battle in which the South's famed River Defense Fleet was virtually eliminated. Memphis! Only two hundred miles up the river, with nothing of any consequence to interfere with the inevitable move down the Mississippi to where we sat, high on the yellow clay bluffs. And still optimism reigned. "Never Vicksburg," everyone said. "Impossible!"

General Beauregard ordered all cotton burned to keep it out of Yankee hands. Plantations were set on fire, and all baled cotton, wherever it stood, was ignited. Packed cotton burns slowly, issuing clouds of reeking smoke. Sometimes I could not glimpse the sun through the thick, gray blanket.

Although it had become plain how fragile human safety was, I was surprised to find myself actually missing the cave we had left behind. In this new and overwhelming estate of ours there was no place a cave could be dug. The front lawn stretched green and smooth out to the roadway, and in back, since we were almost at the top of the hill, the land was nearly level for almost a mile. There were no convenient slopes in which to dig.

I said something of this to Amanda, and her prompt reply was, "There's the cellar, Miss Rosemary."

"The cellar? Oh yes. The cellar. I've never been down there."

"Then come and see. Best put one of my aprons on. It's not right clean down there."

Followed by Betsy, we descended steep, narrow steps leading from the kitchen, and found ourselves in an enormous basement. One long wall was covered with wine racks, on which a goodly number of unopened bottles were laid, making me think less guiltily of the two that Hector had confiscated. In every corner huddled stacks of discarded furniture, baskets of chipped dishes and glassware, rusting tools—all the outgrown or overused household oddments that gather through the years. And Amanda was quite right: it was not clean.

"It's filthy!" I exploded.

"But it is *here*," Amanda said mildly. "We can clean it, and we don't need the whole place. Just room for some mattresses is about all we need."

I looked around. The place was dank, dirty, and thoroughly uninviting, but it had thick walls, a firm wooden floor, and what appeared to be a sturdy ceiling.

"Well," I said doubtfully, "I suppose it might be safer than the rooms abovestairs if things get ..." I paused, not wanting to alarm Betsy, although she was certainly aware that we were living in the midst of a war.

"If things get red hot," Amanda supplied. "That what you mean?"

"Yes, I expect that's what I mean."

We started working and what a chore it was! Supplied with a rag tied to the end of a broom handle, Betsy swept cobwebs down, delighted when she found an impressively large one. Amanda and I tried to concentrate all the discarded household goods in one area, lifting, tugging, shoving, and piling the heavy containers.

"Why don't we just throw these things out?" I grumbled.

"They're not ours, Miss Rosemary. Besides, there could come a time we'll be mighty glad we have them. Best not to throw anything away for a spell."

"You're right, Amanda, of course. Why do I never think of such things myself?"

"You do." Amanda chuckled. "How about when you made those blue slippers for Miss Mary Byrd out of your old coat? I heard you then; you were the one talking about saving and making do."

"Well, perhaps. But I don't know what I should have done without you these past two years."

"Might be I smoothed down a few edges for you, that's about all. But I'm right glad you feel that way, because there is something I've been hankering to ask you."

"Anything, Amanda. What is it?"

She straightened her back, wiped her hands on her apron, and looked squarely at me. "I've been thinking, wondering how you'd feel—you and Mr. Derek—if Betsy and I moved in here with you." With a small grin she added, "I doubt we'd be real crowded."

"Oh, Amanda, I'd like that! You mean you and Betsy and Hector would stay right here? You wouldn't leave at night?"

"Just Betsy and me. Mr. Stafford, he wants Hector to do some building and changing around in the basement under the office. Hector will most likely stay right there."

"Oh dear! Did that fire they had do a lot of damage? I thought it was just a small one."

"This is nothing to do with the fire. This is just some kind of work Mr. Stafford wants done in his basement." I thought her tone was a little odd. "Then Betsy and I can move in here?" she added.

"Yes, Amanda."

"Thank you, Miss Rosemary. You want to take the other end of this basket? We'll slide it over here out of the way."

When Derek came home I told him about the new arrangement. Then I took him downstairs and showed him what we had accomplished.

"It's not very beautiful," I said, "but we are fortunate to have it."

"We may be inviting half the neighbors in! You're clever to have thought of it."

Unfortunately I cannot lie. "It was Amanda's idea."

"Then she is clever and you are brave, because I know you dislike dirt and spiderwebs."

"Betsy took care of the spiderwebs."

He laughed and rumpled my hair. "Well, whatever part you had in it, I compliment you. I'll wrestle some mattresses down here, and we had better put mosquito netting around them. This is the ideal climate for raising mosquitoes."

Over the next few days, the cellar came to seem less appalling, though never appealing. By hanging curtains from the strong rafters we divided the space into three cubicles, one for Amanda and Betsy, one for Derry, and one for me. Home sweet home!

July-December 1862

THE SUMMER OF 1862 WAS HOTTER THAN I HAD EVER imagined weather could be. Mary Byrd and I dispensed with our corsets and as many of our petticoats as decency permitted. We read and heard of Northern troops, unused to the suffocating heat of the South, who fell dead from sunstroke after exerting themselves. Some of their horses, ridden hard, dropped to the ground and never rose again.

With true Southern optimism many people had something to say about these tragedies. "We don't even have to fight 'em. Just sit 'em out in the middle of a Mississippi plantation for a spell and there won't be any Yankees left." Or, "We Southerners must be real hellions, already prepared for our final end." And, "By the time cool weather comes back, there won't be any Yanks around to enjoy it."

And yet the Union Army, under the guidance of Ulysses Simpson Grant, continued to add one Northern victory to another. In September and October they took the towns of Perryville in Kentucky and Iuka and Corinth in Mississippi. It was impossible to glance at a copy of the stubborn little *Citizen*, printed on whatever paper was available, without learning of the inexorable progress of the North.

In October we read that one Lieutenant-General John Clifford Pemberton had been given the responsibility of defending Vicksburg. There was great consternation.

"Why, the man was born and raised in Philadelphia!"

"True, but they say his sympathies are with the South. He married a Southern girl, you know, a Martha Thompson from Norfolk."

"That's all very well, but I don't think we ought to trust him. He may be a Yankee spy!"

A Yankee he may have been, but a spy he was not. After a careful look at the defenses that stretched from Snyder's Bluff, some ten miles north, to Port Hudson, many miles south in Louisiana, he declared himself dissatisfied. Frantic activity followed this pronouncement. Additional batteries and fortifications were built on the hills and along the river. Trees and even buildings that might obstruct the line of fire were removed. Words I had never heard, such as "redoubt" and "earthworks," became familiar as I saw these defenses being dug or erected wherever I looked.

Pemberton's efforts, described in *The Citizen* as "handling the problem of rendering our position impregnable," heartened almost everyone. To me the work was frightening, since it underscored the fact that General Pemberton thought that sooner or later Vicksburg would become the scene of bloodshed. Can any city be made "impregnable"? It seemed as if we would soon find out. In November General Grant succeeded in establishing troops on the far side of the river, a bit to the north, at a place called Milliken's Bend. There was some light shelling.

"He just wants us to know he's there," people said. "He's just sending over his calling card."

And then, in December, came news that delighted Vicksburg. It seemed that General Grant had chosen a place called Holly Springs, not far away, in which to hide supplies of arms and ammunition, and quantities of provisions, where they would be available when needed. Major General Van Dorn, who, people said, was "so thoroughly a Mississippian that he had river water in his veins," learned that a scant fifteen hundred men were stationed at Holly Springs. Van Dorn's thirty-five hundred Confederate horsemen gathered in the woods that surrounded the place and waited quietly for dawn. Then, with the terrifying scream known as the rebel yell, they swept into Holly Springs from every direction. They torched the ammunition dumps, the trains and storage sheds, and the provision depots, rounding up and capturing most of the men who were intended to defend the place.

Every soldier in Vicksburg and every small boy practiced his rebel yell for days, and told and retold the story.

"That's going to set old Mr. Grant back a few steps," they said. "Took away all his pretty guns and bullets and hardtack and potatoes! Now what's old Useless going to do?"

Even I, with my split loyalty, felt pride in the spirited defiance of this Confederate success.

And again Derry suggested—more urgently than before—that I leave the city. "Heaven knows what is to come, Tad, but it is not going to be pleasant."

"And just where do you think of sending me?"

"Uncle Will feels that if we could get you to Boston, Jeffrey Howard's family would happily take you in."

I almost laughed. But of course Derry didn't know of my last meeting with Jeff. "No," I said. "I have no intention of leaving. Vicksburg took me in, all my friends are here. If you leave I will go with you, but not otherwise. And please, Derry, don't ask me again. I shan't change my mind."

My brother has a way of lowering his head slightly and gazing full at one with those dark blue eyes. He did so now. After a long moment he spoke.

"All right, little sister. We'll see this through together." He put his arm around me and kissed my forehead. "I'm really very glad I have you, Tad. You're a special person."

December 1862–April 1863

IT WAS A GRIM CHRISTMAS. WITH SO FEW WARES TO BE had, many of the shopkeepers had locked their doors and gone; some to join the army, others to get along from day to day as well as they could. I made a pair of carpet slippers for Derry, or, more correctly, blue-coat slippers, and a pair of blue-coat mittens for Mary Byrd to wear when riding or driving the buggy in crisper weather. For Betsy, whom Amanda was teaching to read, I found a book I had been fond of as a young girl, buried in the depths of one of our boxes. You would have thought it pure gold from the pride she took in it.

"My own book!" she kept saying, smoothing the cover with her little brown hand. "Betsy's very own book!"

And the year turned, and we continued to read of battles, and we tried to go on living as normally as possible.

In April, such a beautiful month, filled with new growth and birdsong and blossoms, Mary Byrd announced she was going to have a birthday party for me.

"It's just plain silly to sit around waiting to be attacked," she said decisively. "All these sweet little old soldiers need something to amuse them a mite. And I met two who will play music for us—just a fiddle, of course, with the piano—but we can dance and have a happy time and forget all this war nonsense!"

"Are you sure you want to go to all that bother?" I asked.

"Parties are never a bother; parties are what we need! I don't know what we'll find as a collation, but Papa says he still has a good bit of wine—though he always insists it must be watered down for us poor females. I suppose he thinks I might become flown and do something shocking and maybe I will—I'm ripe to, Rosemary—but you and Derek must be there, in your very finest clothes, and we'll laugh and chatter and pay no mind to anything serious! So you will both come, won't you? To your own birthday party?"

"Of course we'll come, and I shall put flowers in my hair and Derry will wear his fanciest frilled shirt, and you're a genius to think of it! It's precisely what we all need, and we'll have a wonderful time."

And we did. There were twenty or so young people in the room when Derry and I arrived, most of whom we knew, and ten or so older folk, including Mr. and Mrs. Blair, of course, and Uncle William, looking quite dashing in his well-fitted evening clothes. Of all the men, only he and Mr. Blair and Derry were not in uniform. The sharp black and white of their attire stood out like exclamation marks.

The talk was all of the South's victories, its high spirits and fighting ability, the courage of its young men, and the impossibility of any serious damage being done to Vicksburg.

"We can just sit up here and watch those Yankees lose the war to our brave boys in gray," one older woman said. "Nothing can touch us here." She flicked a cold glance in Derek's direction, and her lips pursed. "Of course," she added in a voice designed to reach my brother's ears, "if those contemptible young men who stay at home in comfort would get themselves in the army where they belong, this would all be over that much sooner."

Furious, I opened my mouth to speak and was stopped by Derek's hand gripping my shoulder. "Oh no, you don't, Tad."

"But did you hear what she said?" I whispered sharply. "And she intended you to hear it!"

"I know. And it isn't the first time. It won't be the last, either. But you will only make it worse if you say anything."

Fuming, I turned away from that outspoken creature to find Mary Byrd at my side.

"Pay her no mind, Rosemary," she said quietly, and her clear blue eyes were blazing. "Nor you, Derek." She laid her hand on Derry's sleeve, and I saw him cover it with his own.

"Don't concern yourself," he said. "Tonight is a party, and we are here to enjoy ourselves." His voice was serious, but he smiled slightly.

"She is an impossible woman!" Mary Byrd said. "I wish she had never come here."

"She has a right to her opinion, Mary Byrd."

"But she doesn't need to give it so rudely! She doesn't need to give it at all!" Mary Byrd's lips folded together and her eyes were focused on Derry's face.

My brother took her hand, holding it firmly in both of his. A small tight smile played around his mouth.

"This is a party, remember?" he said softly. "As the Scots say, 'Dinna fash yersel'.' Put it quite out of your mind, as I already have."

Ben Fraser suddenly appeared beside us. "What are you three in such deep discussion over?" he asked. "We're wasting all that high-steppin' music from the other room."

"Just what we had decided ourselves," Derek said easily. "Mary Byrd?"

She lifted her chin, put on her best smile, and took his arm. "It's wartime," she said, "and it's wrong to waste anything."

Together they walked through the wide archway and joined the dancers who dipped and spun and circled the floor. Ben and I watched them for a moment.

"Well?" said Ben. I smiled and nodded slightly. "Come along then, my little English lady. At last I can put my strong arm around you! I'll show you dancin' like you never saw!"

After that it was an evening of sheer delight. I danced with all the young men there, but most often with Benjamin. His arm was indeed strong, guiding me through steps so intricate I was amazed that I could manage them. He chatted away, gentle nonsense that made me laugh; he brought me glasses of wine. When I sipped the first one I exclaimed unthinkingly:

"Good heavens! It's not watered!"

"I devoutly hope not! Why should it be watered?"

"Oh, Mary Byrd feared her father might think it more seemly for young women to have a weaker potion. As she put it, 'We might become flown and do something shocking.'"

"What a splendid idea! Do you think *you* might 'become flown and do something shocking'?"

I laughed. "Highly unlikely. We British are a stuffy breed, you know."

"What a shame! I was hoping you might throw yourself into my arms and beg to run away with me."

"It's hardly worth it. We couldn't run very far; you have to be back on duty in the morning."

"What an unromantic female you are! And with those strange eyes—what color are they, Rosemary?"

I gazed full up at him. "They're cat's eyes," I said.

"By heaven, they are! Large—and round—and golden—and hypnotic!"

In fun I widened my eyes and stared straight into his. "I can make you do my bidding just by looking at you," I said in what I hoped was an enticing, mysterious voice.

There was suddenly an odd expression in Ben's hazel eyes, serious and warning. His voice was very soft. "Rosemary, if you look at me like that I am going to kiss you right here in front of everyone!"

Embarrassed, I turned my head away. "I'm sorry," I murmured. "It was just in fun."

"Your eyes are a potent weapon. Be careful how you use them, lady. Now come and dance with me so I can at least hold you."

I found the evening quite exciting. Apparently Derek enjoyed it, too. He barely spoke on the way home, just smiled in the moonlit dark. As he unlocked our door something small and white fell to the floor. I picked it up—an envelope.

"Light a candle, Derry. I want to see what this is." And knew immediately. I looked at the delicate printing of my name on the envelope, quickly tore it open, and drew out the card. Holding it close to the candle I read, "To wish you a shining eighteenth birthday." There was a beautifully executed miniature drawing of Woof, tail wagging furiously, carrying the same basket he had arrived in two years ago. A tiny tag on the handle read, "To Rosemary from Jeff," and from the basket itself spilled flowers, packages—and hearts. In the bottom corner, in the smallest script imaginable, were the words, "I wish I were there. J."

Slowly I undressed and went to bed. I held the card in my hand all night long.

May 1863

I AM GLAD I HAD THAT APRIL EVENING TO REMEMBER.

On May 1 General Grant's Union troops took the town of Port Gibson, to the south of us.

On May 12 he took Raymond, to the east of us.

On May 14 he went on to Jackson, the capital, taking that, too.

On May 16 it was Champion Hill, where Mr. Blair and Ben's father had their plantations.

On May 17 there was the battle of Black Ridge, barely ten miles east of us, and Black Ridge, too, was taken. The sound of gunfire carried on the air.

For the next few days the streets of Vicksburg were filled with Southern soldiers retreating from those battles. Watching them, my heart ached. Thin, bone-weary, dirty, some wearing blood-soaked bandages, they were like stray dogs. And yet they attempted to march rather than shamble as they observed the people watching them. With effort they straightened their backs and held their heads a little higher.

Derry and I stood on one of our galleries. "The great General Pemberton's army," he said. "Nothing stands between the city of Vicksburg and the Yankees now save these men. And they are defeated already!"

"I don't think so," I said. "They are Southerners, they are proud, and they are fighting for what they think is right. They will go on fighting as long as one of them is alive to fire a gun."

"Which may not be very long if Grant attacks Vicksburg."

"As he is bound to do," I said quietly. "How did Mr. Blair and Ben's father manage at Champion Hill? Was there much damage to their plantations?"

Derry looked at me. "Think, Tad!" His tone was crisp. "The fields were undoubtedly burned, possibly most or all of the buildings, too. And do you suppose for one moment the slaves just stayed right there? I do not."

I felt as if I had been hit very hard. "But where would they go? And what would happen to the plantation owners?"

"The slaves, in most cases, simply follow the army. They have no other means of survival. Some of them run wild, filled with a false notion of freedom. They steal, they loot, on occasion they kill. As for the plantation owners, unless they have another source of income, or a great deal of money safely banked—and who knows how safe banks are at this time—they are ruined."

"You mean ... Mr. Blair has *nothing* anymore?"

"He has the house here in Vicksburg, of course, and probably some money in the bank."

"And Ben's father, too?"

"That's right."

"But they still own that land, don't they? The plantations?"

"Unless someone else comes along and simply takes it. What use is it anyway? Without slaves, how can it be worked? There are hundreds of acres there, Tad. It's not like a kitchen garden one or two men can handle."

It was hard for me to grasp. "You mean ... they're not ... not *rich* anymore?"

"That's what I mean."

"Oh, poor Mary Byrd! Where will she get all the pretty things she loves so much?"

"I have hoped for some time that she might let me provide them for her." He smiled and looked straight at me. "If I were her husband, of course."

I stared at him. "Her *husband*?"

"Yes, Tad. You know, marriage?"

My poor brain was whirling. "You want to marry Mary Byrd?"

"Precisely."

"Oh, Derry!"

He sounded almost fearful. "Is that all you can say? 'Oh, Derry'?"

I could feel a great smile moving my lips. "Oh, no! That's not all! It's—it's perfect! I'm so happy for you!"

His deep sigh sounded relieved. "That's better."

"Have you asked her?"

"Not yet. The right time is not just yet."

"Promise to tell me the minute you do." I slipped both arms around his waist and hugged him. "And don't wait long. I'm not terribly reliable about keeping secrets."

I kissed his cheek very quickly and went off, almost dancing, to help Amanda prepare whatever our evening meal would consist of.

* * *

At twilight a band on the hill by the courthouse began to play. I heard the strains of "Dixie" and "Bonnie Blue Flag," and then, from all around the city, the imperative beat of drums.

"They're trying to rally the scattered army," Derry said. "This is the beginning of the end."

We have gone into the basement for the night. After all I have seen and heard today I cannot seem to fall asleep. I have lighted a stub of candle and sit here writing in this confused record I have been keeping for the past three weeks or so. I see that I started writing the day a piece of shell came through the kitchen wall and cut Betsy's head. We learned later that it was probably one of the many practice shells that were fired when the Union troops were striving to fix the proper range. Perhaps this was not the range they were after, because (thank heaven!) nothing has come near us since. Betsy's head is totally healed, and Amanda and Hector covered the gap in the kitchen wall with discarded canvas, held in place by a few well-secured boards. There has been so much destruction that boards are easy to come by.

Derry is sound asleep. I can hear his regular breathing through the curtain. Betsy's, too. Amanda is singing sadly and quietly as she does much of the night. Hymns.

Late May 1863

IT IS LATE MAY IN THIS LONGEST YEAR OF OUR LORD 1863, and the city is under siege. Food has become the most critical problem. With the river blockade well established, nothing comes into Vicksburg and nothing leaves. We are blessed by having a little milk almost every day from friends of Derek's who own a cow. They keep it hidden, knowing it could well be stolen to provide meat. I make sure Betsy gets some of the precious milk, the rest Amanda and I use trying to make something edible from rice flour, which is virtually all we have. No matter what we do, the result is patties as hard as bricks, or a horrible sticky paste.

Ben Fraser stopped here this morning and I was shocked into silence at the change in him! Looking at the pale, thin, exhausted young man it was impossible to find the healthy, flirtatious Ben who had danced with me at Mary Byrd's little more than a month ago. I asked him in and he sank wearily into an armchair.

"I am so tired," were his first words. "Have you anything to eat?" were the second.

I knew how little there was, but I fetched a bowl of the cornmeal gruel that Amanda makes, poured a few drops of milk on it, and added a few grains of sugar and a scraping of nutmeg. What a poor dish to offer! But Ben clutched it to him, spooning the soft, warm mixture into his mouth as if he had not eaten for days. Perhaps he had not.

"What supplies we have must last out the siege," he said. "No new supplies can reach us."

"It is so hard to believe," I murmured.

A little color had returned to his face since he had eaten, and perhaps a little strength to his body, too, for he sat a trifle straighter.

"Vicksburg is completely ringed by Union troops, Rosemary," he explained. "You must know that."

"Yes. I know it."

"The Union general, William Tecumseh Sherman, is in charge of the army that starts north of us at the river and swings around to the east. McPherson's army starts where Sherman's ends, curving south where it meets McClernand's men. Then General Lauren's division forms the lower part of the arc, swinging west to the Mississippi."

"Like a giant archery bow," I said, "with the river as the cord. The bow loops in a semicircle, enclosing Vicksburg."

"Exactly." His eyes lifted wearily to mine and suddenly there were tears in them. "Dear Lord in heaven, Rosemary, why did you ever come here? Or why did you not leave when you could have? Now there is no way out of the trap. Every road is blocked, the river is controlled for four hundred miles, the railroads have been destroyed, and every Confederate bridge is gone. *Why* didn't you leave?"

His intensity shook me. "Derek asked me to. I couldn't run away. If you, and the others who have befriended me, can stand it, so can I."

His voice came as a whisper. "I hope to God that *I* can."

Instinctively I moved to comfort and soothe him as I would a frightened child. But perhaps I had not been meant to hear those words. Ben glanced at me, then wiped his hand roughly across his face and stiffened his back.

"It can't be long now," he said.

"You mean ... for Vicksburg to be ... taken?" He nodded. "How long?"

"Only until there are no Confederate troops left to fight."

"But surely the Union troops will suffer as much in battle."

"Not true. The Yanks have built roads behind their lines so everything they need is constantly arriving. They have the river; their boats can come and go as they choose. The Yanks lack for nothing, my dear. We *have* nothing."

"Except spirit."

"Spirit is cold comfort to an empty belly." He rose slowly and stretched. "I must go, Rosemary. From the bottom of my heart I thank you for the food." He took my hand. "May God keep you safe," he murmured. When he kissed my fingers his lips were cold.

When Derry came home this afternoon Hector was with him. After Hector had greeted me and gone toward the kitchen to see Amanda and Betsy, I told Derek about Ben Fraser's visit.

"He was so hungry! I never thought people could be that hungry!"

"If there is anything less than a minimum," my brother said, "that's what the troops are getting. Uncle Will has closed the law office because, he says, the citizens of Vicksburg have more important things on their minds than legal matters. Like starving, for instance."

"You mean he has just locked the office up and left it? What if someone does want a lawyer?"

"Remember Uncle Will lives right above the office, Tad. If anyone wants him, he is there."

"Did he and Hector finish the work in the basement?" I asked idly.

Derek's eyes fastened on mine. "What do you know about the work in the basement?"

"Why, only that Amanda told me Hector was going to help Uncle Will do some building or something. Should I know more?"

There was a pause before his answer. "I'm not sure. I shall have to think a bit. But there is something else I want to tell you. If the office is going to be closed for a while, I must find something to do with myself. I can't just sit all day twirling my thumbs. So—I was thinking I might offer my help in one of the hospitals in the city."

I looked up at him. "But what would you do?"

"Tad, do you remember when I used to go with Father on many of his calls? He even took me with him to the hospital fairly often. I used to watch everything he did, everything the nurses did. I had just about decided to study medicine as soon as I was old enough. Then, when I *was* old enough, Uncle Will asked me to join him here and become a lawyer. The thought of going to America was so exciting that the idea of becoming a doctor couldn't compare with it." Derry rose and wandered around the room. "But a lot of hospital procedure is familiar to me—I could do most bandages, I think, and probably set a broken bone, and I know a little about certain medicines—but, oh, I don't know! Would it be silly of me, Tad, to inquire whether I might be of use in one of the hospitals?"

He turned back, facing me, and the eight years between us made no difference. He really wanted my opinion.

So I gave it. "I think it would be a very sensible thing to do. If you are not needed, someone will certainly tell you, but it seems to me that anyone with even a touch of medical knowledge or ability would be welcomed with open arms! You must have read in *The Citizen* today that the two hospitals in Vicksburg are so full that some large warehouses are being prepared to receive patients. Surely there is a need for people to take care of them."

He looked at me closely for a minute, and then grinned. Leaning down, he gave me one of his light kisses on my hair. "Bless you! Tomorrow morning I'll try my luck. Now it must be almost time for dinner—if we can call what we eat these days 'dinner.' I had better wash up." He started from the room, then turned back. "Ask Hector and Amanda to bring Betsy and join us on the veranda later. There are several things we should talk about. And tell Hector to bring another of those bottles that don't belong to us. A little wine may fill some of the spaces in our stomachs."

It was a beautiful evening. Amanda and I sat in rocking chairs, Derry threw a cushion on the veranda floor for himself, and Hector leaned his massive body against one of the pillars. Betsy chased fireflies across the yard, Woof romping beside her. It was so quiet. Just sleepy bird sounds and the small noises of humans going about their business.

"If it could just stay this way," I said. "This beautiful, this quiet."

"Let's pretend it will," Derry replied. "Stop guarding that wine, Hector, and we'll drink a toast." Hector worked the cork from a dusty bottle and poured a rosy liquid into the four glasses. As Derry handed them round, he said, "A toast. To peace. To the swift end of the war, and peace."

"Please, God," Amanda added softly.

The wine was soft on my tongue. I leaned back and set the rocking chair moving slowly. "Derry, you said there were things we should talk about. What are they?"

"Well, for one, I think it's time you knew more about Hector, and why he came to America. Why he didn't stay on that good farm."

"Oh yes! I've been wanting to know. It was Liberia, wasn't it, Hector?"

"That's right. Liberia." He took a drink of his wine and sat a moment, gazing out across the grass. "Well, I told you about the prince, and all the years he was a slave to Mr. Foster down in Natchez. I told you about Mr. Foster finding a wife for Prince, and how they had a passel of young 'uns. And most of the young 'uns, they were slaves, too. But some got away—they came to Liberia. Well, Prince's first grandchild was Simon. Born in Liberia, Simon was, the same year as me. Eighteen-twenty, that was. So there were those fifty years that Prince was a slave, and his children after him, and then Prince got his freedom and he wanted nothing more than to go back to his own country. But he was an old man by then, and not as strong as he once was. Tall, yes, and straight, and—well, sort of *noble* looking. That's the only word I can find." Hector paused, his eyes seeing some faraway picture. Softly I spoke.

"But he *did* get back. You told me so."

"Yes, he got back. He landed in Monrovia—that's the big city in Liberia—but he never went farther. He died a few months later." Hector lifted his chin, leaning his head back against the white pillar. "Simon and I were nine years old the first time I saw the prince. I'll never forget that. Soon after he landed, it was. There was a man! There were always children around him. A heap of children. He didn't talk much, but one day he looked straight at me with his sad black eyes, and he put his hand on my head and shook it a little—and he smiled at me. A sad smile. I felt like Jesus Himself had touched me. I'd have done anything he asked me to do. But he never asked. No, he never asked. He was there only three, four months before he died. He never got to his own country. Prince!"

There were unashamed tears in the man's eyes. Derek picked up the wine bottle and refilled our glasses, giving Hector a few moments to collect himself. Amanda gazed at her husband, her eyes filled with love. Betsy came across the grass and settled down by her mother's chair, Woof stretching out beside her.

"Well," said Hector after a bit, "Simon and I stayed good friends. He used to tell me all the tales his family had told him, about how slaves were treated by some of the masters, and about how Prince had worked to be free—oh, we talked ourselves out in those days. And the more I heard that word 'slave,' the more I hated it. And Simon told me about people who tried to help some of the slaves escape to places where they could be free folks. And somehow I knew that was what I had to do. Get myself to America, to where the slaves were, and find ways to help them get free. So I worked at anything anybody would pay me for, and when I was twenty and had a little money in my pocket, Simon and I, we said goodbye, and I got myself on a ship and came here. And in the hold of that ship were black men chained together, and seems to me they swore and wept the whole way across the ocean. And when I listened to them I was the angriest free black man you ever saw!"

He gave a bitter chuckle and tipped the last of his wine down his throat.

"You went first to Natchez, didn't you?" Derek asked.

"Yes, I went to Natchez. That was about the only place I knew to go. I found the plantation that used to belong to Mr. Foster, and it had a new owner and the fields were full of slaves and I was sick in my heart. So mostly I stayed in the towns, where I could always find some sort of paying job, and I listened and I learned. I learned about the folks, black ones and white ones, who were doing what they could to set some of those slaves free. They had to get them to Canada or as far north in the States as they could, or on a ship to Liberia. And I learned about the Underground Railroad, and before I knew it, I was part of it all."

"What is the Underground Railroad, Hector?" I asked. I had not heard the term before.

"Not the kind of railroad you know, Miss Rosemary, with tracks and trains. Mostly it was ways across woods and fields, it was river crossings where small boats hid in the night, waiting to help. It was lonely houses and little churches, sometimes a single light burning in a window to mark it out, and the people in those houses, black folks and white alike, they took in the runaways and kept them through the daylight until it was dark again. Sometimes there were tunnels dug under the buildings—many a tunnel I helped to dig. In fact ..." Hector stopped speaking suddenly and his eyes moved quickly to Derry.

"We might as well tell her," my brother said.

"Tell me what?"

"That there is an escape tunnel leading from this house."

"From *this* house? Impossible! I'd have seen it."

"A secret tunnel anyone could see wouldn't be much use. The entrance to it is behind the shelves where the wine is stored—one set of shelves swings out. Hector knows. He helped to dig it."

"Where does it go?" I asked, looking at Hector.

"Under the fields away from this house. After near a mile it ends in thick woods."

"How did you come to work on it?"

"Mr. Bartlett, who owns this house, he's a friend of Mr. Stafford's. I was working round the law office one day when Mr. Bartlett asked me if I could do some work for him. Mr. Stafford said for me to go ahead and next thing I knew I was up here digging that tunnel."

I was sitting straight in my chair, my mind whirling. "The Bartletts had an escape tunnel? I can't believe it! Remember, Derry, Mary Byrd said they were one of the finest families in Vicksburg?"

My brother chuckled. "I remember. And I agree. It was a brave thing to do. But the Bartletts were not the only ones. Shall I tell you about the cellar under Uncle Will's office?"

"Not Uncle Will, too!"

"Uncle Will, too. Before Vicksburg was cut off so decisively, slaves could wait in that cellar with reasonable safety until a boat came that would carry them north. Often when they were put on board they were wrapped in sacking to look like bales of cotton."

I was speechless. All this going on about me, and I had never guessed! Then another thought struck me. Hector, Mr. Bartlett, Uncle Will ...

"What happens to people who are caught helping slaves escape?"

"There is a Fugitive Slave Act," Derry said, "and efforts are made to enforce it, but they haven't been very successful. That's why the Bartletts left Vicksburg. The Slave Act enforcers were a bit too close to them, so they went to Ohio to do what they could for runaways who made it that far. That's how we got this house, too. I already knew about the tunnel. The Bartletts had no need to worry."

"And is that why Uncle Will closed his office? So the . . . the enforcers wouldn't find that basement?"

"No. There actually isn't any business for us now. Not in law, and not in helping fugitive slaves."

I was filled with questions. "How could the slaves who were trying to escape get to Uncle Will's? They couldn't simply walk through town, knock on his door, and say, 'May I hide in your cellar?' "

Hector laughed. "There are a heap of little coves in the riverbank below Vicksburg. Some dark nights I'd take a rowboat down there and listen for a signal—a special low whistle. Then I'd pull in close and they'd scramble aboard and we'd row back upriver, and Mr. Stafford would be watching. I'd open a door that is half underwater and they'd wade through and climb a great high ladder and be in that basement." He paused and sighed. "It used to give me a good feeling. It surely did. But in Vicksburg that's all over now. No way into the city and no way out."

For a moment I sat in stunned silence, trying to absorb it all. Then I turned to Derry. "You helped, I know you did. What did you do?"

He spoke quietly. "Whatever I could. When Uncle Will was out I took his place and watched. I took care of the cuts and scrapes and sprains and sometimes broken bones the slaves got pushing through thick woods in the dark—or when they were beaten before running away. Just ... whatever I could. They'd break your heart, Tad."

There was a great lump in my throat. I could say nothing.

"Mr. Stafford, he's gotten a lot away from here," Hector said. "If they make it to Ohio, there are Indians there—Ottawas, they're called—and others in New York and Massachusetts to help them on the freedom path. Sometimes runaways are caught, and we won't talk about what happens to them. But hundreds have made it, and I've been blessed by being part of that, and all because of Prince. I know he's up there in God's heaven, looking down, and I pray he smiles."

Hector leaned back, his eyes lifted to the sky. I felt the strongest urge to look upward, too, and see a strong, dark face. With a smile.

Early June 1863

IT IS JUNE NOW, AND THIS STRANGE LIFE GOES ON. WE seem to get three quiet times each day. The first occurs about eight o'clock in the morning, the second at noontime, and the third at eight in the evening. We assume the troops are either allowing their guns to cool, or are having a meal, or both. In any case it is reasonably safe to emerge from our houses at these times.

The morning after Derry's and my talk of hospital work, he had gone out early, during the first lull. Amanda and I were dragging the mattresses up the stairs from the cellar and laying them on the grass behind the house. It is a backbreaking chore, but if we don't do so, we lie all night on damp, musty-smelling pallets. It is a wonder that we sleep at all, save that sheer exhaustion—of both the body and the spirit—can be a powerful sedative. I am always surprised when I waken to find I am still alive.

As the last mattress was pushed and dragged out into the sun, Derek and Mary Byrd came round the side of the house. I had not seen her in several days, and I stared in amazement. Her hair was covered with a drab kerchief, and the tendril or two that showed were dull. Deep shadows stood out on her pale face, hollowing her cheeks but emphasizing the blue of her eyes. Her limp frock was hidden under a patched apron she must have borrowed from one of the servants, and on her feet she wore an incongruous pair of pink carriage boots, edged with white fur. It would have been hard to find the exquisite Mary Byrd in this forlorn girl if it had not been for the sparkle in the dark-fringed eyes and the beautiful quick smile.

"Rosemary!" she said. "Has Derek told you? We're going to work in a hospital."

"You?" I gasped. The thought of my butterfly friend coping with the pain and blood and horrors that I knew existed in every hospital was impossible to accept. "Both of you?"

"No, not both of us. All three of us, for Derek says they need as many hands as they can get."

"I'd be glad to come," I said quickly. "But will I really be of any use? I've never even been in a hospital."

"You took care of Mamma for years," Derek pointed out. "You have two hands, two eyes, and a brain. You'll be of use."

I looked down at my bare feet. "I have no shoes."

Mary Byrd lifted one foot and waggled it. "You see what I'm wearing? You must have something you can put on. Let's look in that magical English trunk of yours."

She grasped my hand and pulled me into the house to where the old trunk stood in my bedroom. She lifted the lid and rummaged through the contents, discarding heavy woolen clothing, knitted mufflers, and mittens, until, in triumph, she pulled out a pair of Wellington boots I had not seen in years.

"There! What did I tell you? I knew we'd find something! Put them on. Do they still fit you?"

I stood looking at those old boots, once worn by a young Rosemary Monica Stafford Leigh while playing in rain-wet English grass. Rosemary Monica, taught so carefully by a loving mother to always dress appropriately and with quiet good taste. I started to giggle.

"If you can wear pink carriage boots I can wear Wellingtons: the footwear chosen by the best-dressed young ladies all over the world! But not to be worn on bare feet."

It took Mary Byrd only a moment to find a pair of heavy knitted socks, which she handed me. "These must once have been Derek's, but they'll do. Are there any old sheets we can take, Rosemary? Derek says linen for dressings is in short supply."

As I pulled the socks on my feet and struggled into the boots, I told her where to look for linen, and a moment or two later we were back outdoors with Derry. He looked with absurdly popping eyes at my feet and exclaimed solemnly, "It's Cinderella, as I live and breathe!"

Many of the larger buildings in the city, and a few of the homes, have been converted into hospitals for Confederate soldiers. The Union wounded are loaded onto boats in the river and ferried to Northern hospitals safely behind the lines where medical care and supplies are available. In the makeshift accommodations in Vicksburg, army doctors, assisted by the few local practitioners, do what they can for the men, but their stores of drugs and medications are melting with dreadful speed and cannot be replenished, because of the total blockade.

The Citizen—and my common sense—had told me all these things, but I was not prepared for the reality. When we stepped through the door of an abandoned warehouse it was like walking into a nightmare. Twenty or so cots were pushed close together, all of them filled, as were mattresses, pallets, and blankets laid on the floor. The smell of blood and vomit so permeated the place I could scarcely breathe. Gray uniforms were stained and torn. Young faces were twisted with pain, young lips bitten through with the effort not to howl like an injured animal. The more fortunate were unconscious. There were few windows to let daylight in, and in dim corners candles had been lit, or twists of rag dipped in oil were burning in saucers. (Sufficient oil for lamps had long been impossible to find.) The few doctors had set up a surgery at one end of the long room, partially screened from view by quilts and rugs hung from the rafters. From behind this enclosure came a scream that froze me in my tracks. Mary Byrd let out a little whimper of anguish. Derek put a firm hand on each of our arms.

"You'll get used to it. I know it's dreadful, but . . ."

A woman approached us, one I had often seen and nodded to in the shops we both patronized. She smiled at Derek.

"You are here, Mr. Leigh. I am so glad. I'm Mrs.

Pepper. I saw you here earlier this morning and one of the doctors told me who you were. And you have brought us more help. How wonderful!"

Derry introduced Mary Byrd and me, and Mrs. Pepper led us to a long table holding various supplies. My knees were shaking. Using a pair of scissors, she neatly cut my mother's hand-embroidered sheets into squares and strips, talking quietly as she worked.

"All the boys are so thirsty. There isn't enough fresh water to let them drink, but if you wet a piece of the linen and wipe their lips with it they say it helps a little."

Leaving a pile of linen squares on the table, she tucked several more into her apron strings, and offered a handful to Mary Byrd and to me. Then she poured a little water into two tin cups and gave us those. My hand was so unsteady the precious water slopped.

"Do what you can," she said. "I'll be around here somewhere if you have questions." She turned to Derry. "You come along this way. From what I was told you may be of help to the doctors."

She led him away and Mary Byrd and I were left standing alone. I was sure she could hear my heart thudding. We looked at each other, I gave a little shrug, Mary Byrd repeated it, and we parted.

Somehow I found myself moving from one figure to another, trying to smile, dampening dry, cracked lips with the cool cloth, wiping sweat from foreheads, remembering how to take a pulse as I had done for Mamma, and trying to make mental notes of those who seemed most in need of immediate attention from the doctors. The air was stifling, and my clothes clung to my perspiring body, but suddenly what I was doing was more important than how I felt. There was a constant low sound of moans and weeping, punctuated by raw screams from the surgery. I turned once to find Derry beside me.

"They shriek so!" I said.

"Yes. There is little to drug them with. Some whiskey, but not much laudanum left. The amputations are the worst. Try not to listen."

Useless advice! As well try not to hear the cries of tortured souls in Hell. Sometimes I became aware of the crashing and whining of the battle outside, and the solid thuds when a building was hit, but all that seemed far away.

Once Mrs. Pepper stopped me as I passed. "Help me change this dressing," she said. "I'll show you how. Throw this soiled bandage in one of those pails against the wall. When anyone has a moment we scrub them out to use again. Now, hold this end of the linen firmly while I wind it—that's right, you're doing nicely. Can you finish this bit? I'll go on. And thank you! You have gifted hands!"

The hours slipped by, and I forgot fatigue, hunger, and even fear. This was the present. Everything outside was either past or future.

That day has set a pattern. Each morning Derry, Mary Byrd, and I go to one hospital or another and spend the day. At night I force myself to eat whatever

Amanda has been able to find, and then I sleep as if I had been poleaxed into witlessness.

Amanda told me that there are skinned rats hanging in the meat market. They and mule meat are all that is available.

Mid-June 1863

IT IS AMAZING WHAT THE HUMAN BODY CAN LIVE through. Without enough food, restorative sleep, or sufficient water for cooking, drinking, and bathing; living with the constant knowledge that at any moment a shell may come whistling down onto (and into!) the house and very likely taking our lives with it—somehow we still manage to go on from minute to minute, from hour to hour, from day to day.

I am torn by pity for the soldiers. I find them lying on our veranda, seeking the shade, so weary that they can sleep anywhere at any time, so hungry some of them are comatose. A few days ago two of them stood gazing in the kitchen window while Amanda was mixing the eternal corn bread. She told me later that when she emptied the batter into a pan and put it in the oven the men pleaded with her to let them scrape the bowl.

"There's nothing there to scrape," she said. "This bowl's as clean as a whistle."

"Please. Look, we have bacon—we'll add that to what's in the bowl. . . ."

Amanda told me she looked at the bacon. It was greasy and green with mold. "It turned my stomach upside down," she said. But she gave them the bowl, they cut up the bacon with their knives, scraping away as much of the mold as they could, added a little water, and boiled the mess into a sort of soup.

"It's easier to swallow than the bread they give us—

made of pea flour, it is, and so dry we can't get it down."

So each morning Amanda leaves a little more batter in the bowl than she ordinarily would, and every day there are a few more boys than the day before. My heart bleeds for them, but my heart bleeds for so many things now. The Union troops are far better fed and supplied and tended than the Confederates, but a dead Northern soldier is just as dead as a dead Southern boy.

Mary Byrd and I arrived at the warehouse hospital this morning just as a crew of litter bearers was bringing in the wounded. Derek had gone to another makeshift hospital, and so was not with us. We hurried in ahead of the injured, trying to make room for the new arrivals in the crowded room.

"Put him down there," I directed two bearers, and they gently placed the stretcher on the floor, lifted the patient, and slid him carefully onto a blanket I had spread. I knelt beside him. His face was grimed and streaked with dirt, he had lost his cap and his hair was matted and darkened with sweat and filth, the right sleeve of his tunic was soaked with blood, and his arm lay limp across his chest.

I wet a cloth with water and started to wipe his face clean, when he spoke.

"Hello, Rosemary. Fancy meeting you here!" A crooked grin touched his mouth.

I stared at his partially cleaned face. "Ben!"

"Sorry not to have tidied up before we met ..."

"Oh, Ben! I'm so glad to see you—and I'm so sorry! It's your arm?"

"I assume it's my arm, although I should be quite happy to give it to anyone who might want it. Don't touch me, Rosemary. I'm a mess."

I didn't bother to answer that. I cleaned his face, wiped some of the muck from his hair, and then fetched scissors to cut away the sleeve of his jacket. Trying to match his strained flippancy I said, "Where have you been spending your time lately? You don't look quite as groomed as usual."

"I believe I spent last night with my head in a dung heap. It was not really of my choosing—I just seemed to land there." He winced as I tried to remove the sleeve from the wound, only to find it stuck tight. Again I went to work with the scissors, as carefully as I could, until I had the flesh freed from the cloth. I could see the white of the bone through the mangled meat of his arm. There had been a time—not long ago—when I would have behaved like any well-bred young lady and fainted, but that time was past.

"It could well be worse," I said, trying to sound encouraging.

"Do you think I will lose it, Rosemary?"

I had become quite knowledgeable during these days of hospital work, and I looked squarely at him. "No, Ben. I don't think so. The bone is broken, but it doesn't seem to be shattered."

"That's nice to hear. I should hate to think I couldn't put my arm about you the next time we dance."

"Try to rest a bit now," I said. "I'll be back as soon as I can."

I got to my feet, taking the ruined sleeve for disposal, and looked down at him. His length stretched on the thin blanket made him seem utterly helpless, and I moved quickly away before he could see the tears that filled my eyes.

From time to time I went back to where Ben lay until at last he was taken into surgery. Then I prayed as hard as I could that he would not lose his arm. God must have heard me, for some time later he was brought out and laid on the blanket to rest. His right arm was splinted, and bandaged—and in place.

It is still June but I neither know nor care the date. The sun lasts longer, and it was still very light when Mary Byrd and I left the hospital during the eight o'clock quiet. Derek set off to see how Uncle Will fared, promising to be home within the hour. With the guns stilled for a while it was astonishing to hear birds singing, as if it were a normal, peaceful Mississippi evening. I said as much to Mary Byrd.

"I know," she said. "I wish *I* could sing through all this! A pair of swallows has built a nest in our parlor chimney at home, and when the thumping from all that firing shakes down part of the nest they just fly down, pick up the pieces, and start making repairs."

"Like the people of Vicksburg," I said. "They don't give up, they just keep rebuilding and going on somehow."

"Seems like we have no choice, honey. We *can't* just give up."

"Many people would," I said. "I would, I think, if I did not have you and Derek to bolster me up."

Mary Byrd glanced at me and smiled. "You think you would, but you're stronger than you know, Rosemary."

My back and legs were so tired from the long day at the hospital that I stumbled as I walked. "I am not at all strong. I am so weary at this very moment I could curl up right here in the roadway and go to sleep!" As I spoke I thought I heard some small sound from one of the caves that line the streets. "What was that? Did you hear it, Mary Byrd?"

"I didn't hear anything."

"There! There it is again! It sounded like a . . . a groan. Like a person groaning."

We stopped, looking around us. The sound seemed to come from a cave dug into the high slope near a house. The entrance was clogged with debris, apparently left by a shell that had plowed across the ground above it.

"In there," I said. "I think there is someone trapped in there!" Holding our breath we listened, and again I heard what was most certainly a groan. "Mary Byrd, we have to do something! To be buried alive under that . . ."

There was not a soul in sight to help us. The sun had almost set, leaving the rose-tinted gray of evening, when—first with a few shots and then more and more—the battle was joined again.

Without a word between us we started trying to scoop out the yellowish clay from the entrance to the cave, using our bare hands. The clay had packed so hard it was impossible to scrape away. I looked frantically through the litter that was everywhere. Broken glass, shingles, some boards from a house that had been struck. I pounced on a board, finding it far heavier than I had expected, but it would have to do. Together Mary Byrd and I pushed one end of the board as far into the clay as we could, and then threw all our weight on the free end, trying to lever the dirt out. With depressing slowness we managed to pry small chunks from the door to the cave. The broken ends of the board were sharp, and splinters scraped and cut our hands. As we pressed with all the strength of our bodies against the end of the board I heard myself grunting with the effort but I could not help it. Push the board as far into the clay as possible, lean all our weight across the bottom of it, pressing the lodged end up and out, scrape the accumulated clay from the board, press it in again. Groans still came from that hideous tomb. Two or three times I shouted, hoping for a word from whoever was buried there, but there was none.

We worked for what seemed like hours. The light was almost gone. We were barely aware of the clamor of the shelling. And then came the moment when we pressed the board against the solid clay and felt it slide through, throwing us forward.

"It went through," I gasped. "There's a hole here now. We can get our hands in. Look!"

Mary Byrd put her face close to the small opening. "Hello, in there! Can you hear us? We'll have you out in a few minutes. Can you hear us?"

There were no answering words, and with a strange burst of renewed energy we scrabbled away at the clay with our hands, pulling larger and larger pieces away until the space was wide enough to crawl through.

"I'm smaller than you are," Mary Byrd managed to say as she struggled for breath. "I'll see if I can get in."

Crouching, she wormed her way awkwardly into the cave, the pink carriage boots pushing and waving, while I prayed the opening would not give way.

"Can you see anything?" I called. "Are you all right?"

"I've found somebody—a woman, I think. I can't see anything. I don't think she's conscious, but she's breathing. Can you reach in, Rosemary? Maybe ... if we both ..."

As she spoke I was on my knees in the mess, my head, shoulders, and arms inside the cave, everything around us reverberating with the whine and crash and thud of shells.

"Where is she? I can't see."

"I'll stretch her arm across to you—there—can you reach her hand?"

"Not quite ..."

"I'm trying to push her closer. There—now try again ..."

Groping, I felt a hand, and my fingers automatically felt for the pulse—weak but steady. I grasped the hand, flaccid in mine, and pulled as gently as I could. I could feel the woman's body moving toward me.

"I'm pushing," Mary Byrd's voice came through the darkness. "I don't want to hurt her any more than she is . . ."

"I know." I shifted my grip to the woman's upper arm, and her body slid across the rough cave floor closer to the opening. "If we can turn her so her head is nearest this hole," I said, gasping so hard for air that I could barely speak, "I think I can pull her out."

Somehow together we turned the heavy, inert shape until I could get both my hands under the armpits and pull. Mary Byrd eased the lower part of the body up and into the entrance and in a moment or two we had the victim stretched out on the roadway. Mary Byrd crawled out and we sat side by side, every breath an effort, our chests heaving, gazing through the almost-dark at the woman who lay before us. An ugly wound had bloodied one side of her head, but there was no sign that she might have been crushed by the weight of the fallen clay, nor did any limbs appear to be broken.

In the sudden light of a shell that exploded not far from us Mary Byrd leaned closer to look at the dirty, bloody face. For a moment she didn't move, then she turned slowly to me.

"Do you know who that is?" she asked.

"No. Who?"

"Mrs. Harrington."

"Who is Mrs. Harrington?"

Mary Byrd's voice was cool and deliberate. "Mrs.

Harrington is the charming lady who announced at my party that if Derek would do his duty and join the army . . ."

"I remember," I said.

Mary Byrd looked at me. "Let's put her back in the cave," she said. And then we stared at each other and broke into uncontrollable, insane, hysterical laughter.

Late June 1863

As HELLISH AS THE HOSPITALS ARE—AND THAT IS PRE-cisely the word for them, hellish, filled with agony and fear, alive with the constant sound of shelling and musket fire from without, and the soul-tearing groans and screams of suffering within—they are in a way self-contained. Once inside one does whatever one can do to ease pain, to soothe fear, to mend broken bodies, to lend a fragment of strength. When I enter it is as if I turn off a large portion of myself and am unaffected by the incredible noise and terror and danger that surrounds us. The hospitals have become familiar to me, almost comforting.

This morning I had something of a shock when I came through the door, for the first person I saw was Uncle Will.

He was on one knee beside a soldier lying on a blanket, sponging away blood from a leg wound. The gray trousers had been neatly slit open. My uncle was smiling at the patient.

"Relax, boy," I heard him say. "Nothing wrong that a week off your feet won't take care of." In return he got a crooked grin from the young man.

"And pray God in a week this may be over, sir," he said.

"Uncle Will! I never thought to see you here."

"Good morning, Rosemary. I seem to have spare time on my hands, so I may as well use it." He turned back to the soldier. "Why do you think it may all be over in a week?" he asked.

"Just something I heard last night—before I got this." He indicated his leg.

"And what was it that you heard?"

"It was a flag officer. He was looking for General Pemberton. Asked me had I seen him."

"And had you?"

"Yes, sir." He looked up at Uncle William with unholy mischief in his eyes. "I'd seen him just a few minutes before. He was comin' out of one of the caves." He paused, then added, "But I didn't say anything about that. Seems like he's got enough trouble without his men ratting on him. Anyhow, this flag officer said he'd heard that Vicksburg would surrender on July fourth. That's not more than a week away, is it, sir?"

"No. Do you have any reason to think this is true? Have you heard of any arrangements for surrender?"

"No, sir, but we don't hear much, you know. Can't imagine old Vicksburg surrendering, but then—I can't imagine going on like this much longer. None of us is in great shape, sir." The grin came back to light his eyes. "The rumble of our stomachs is 'most as loud as the Yankee shelling."

Uncle Will placed a neatly folded square of linen over the wound and tied it with a strip of the same fabric. "That will hold you until one of the doctors takes a look at it," he said, "but don't fret. The wound is clean and it will heal, given a little time."

"Thank you, sir."

Uncle Will gave the young man's shoulder a pat and got to his feet, turning to me.

"Are you all right, Rosemary? I've seen ghosts that looked stronger than you."

"It's the latest fashion among young ladies," I told him. "To be pale, thin, and disheveled is quite in the mode."

"Then you must be one of the leaders, my dear. Is Derek with you?"

"Not this morning. He and Mary Byrd are in another hospital."

"Are they indeed." Uncle Will's eyebrow cocked, and we grinned at each other. "Rosemary," he went on, changing the subject, "has Derek heard anything of a possible surrender?"

"He hasn't mentioned it to me, and I think he would. There has been nothing in *The Citizen* about it. It is hard to imagine the war being over—I can't remember quietness."

"The surrender of Vicksburg would not be the end of the war, my dear, but it would certainly hasten it. And it must come soon. There is no way to get fresh troops into the city, and the men here are starving and sick and exhausted. We are no match for a well-fed, well-supplied Union Army."

"You say, 'we' as if you were a born Mississippian, Uncle."

"I have come to be—or almost. My head tells me the Union cause, the abolishment of slavery, is right. But I am proud of Vicksburg and its courage, and my heart aches for what has been done to it. Well, we mustn't stand here chatting, girl. Come along. Let's get to work." He gave my cheek a quick kiss and was gone.

There was a knock at our door tonight, and when Derry opened it Ben almost fell into the room. His uniform was smeared with dirt and he carried his right arm stiffly. There was a rank smell about him—somehow it seemed the odor of fear. His mouth worked like a child's, and tears streaked his face. Derek helped him to a chair.

"Ben!" he said. "What is it? What's the matter, man?"

Ben rocked back and forth, his good left hand rubbing his eyes, wiping across his mouth, clenching and unclenching.

"I can't go out there again," he mumbled. "I'm scared! I'm so scared! And so hungry. Maybe they'll shoot me for this—I don't care. I don't care about anything anymore. I wish I was dead. I just wish I was safely dead. Don't make me go out there again—I'll go plumb crazy if I have to go out there again! It never stops. The shooting . . . the shelling . . . it never stops!"

As he continued to mutter, half of what he said inaudible, Derry turned to me.

"Stay with him. I'll be right back."

Quickly he moved to the door of his room, reappearing a minute later with a small flask. Uncorking the top, he put his hand gently on Ben's head, tipped it back, and held the flask to his lips.

"Drink," he said firmly. "Take a swallow, Ben. That's the boy."

"What is it?" I asked.

"Brandy."

"Where did you get brandy?"

"I've had it for months. Go on, Ben, take another swallow."

"But what will it do to him?"

"On an empty stomach? I don't know. But it's the only thing I can think of. The man's in shock, Tad. This may help to bring him out of it, or it may put him to sleep. Or, of course, it may make him vomit. We'll just have to see."

Ben pushed the flask away and looked up at Derry, his eyes wide, but somehow clearer.

"Thank you," he said quietly. "I'm sorry. I'm terribly sorry. I never meant ..."

"It doesn't matter, Ben," I said, and knelt beside him.

"Oh yes, it matters. Everything matters. But I can't bear it anymore. It's never going to stop and I can't bear it anymore."

"It will stop, Ben. It will stop—fairly soon now, I think. Could you sleep? Come down in the basement with us. It won't be quite as noisy there. Come along, Derek will help you."

Derek tumbled another mattress down the stairs to the dank, gloomy basement, and between us we managed to get Ben stretched out on it. We removed his stinking jacket, loosened his belt, took off his boots, threw a blanket over him, and stood looking down as his eyes drooped closed. In seconds he was soundly asleep.

I looked at my brother. "What happened to him, Derry? I never thought to see Ben this way."

"People can take only so much. The limit is different in different people, but eventually there comes a moment when it is all too much. Sleep may help him a little. Go to bed yourself, Tad. There is nothing more we can do for him tonight."

I was wakened once when Ben screamed aloud, but he didn't rouse. I left the cellar before he awoke. Derek stayed with him until they both finally came up the stairs, Ben quiet and shamefaced, but more in control of himself.

We said nothing more about it. He left the house after breakfast.

July 2, 1863

IT WAS MIDAFTERNOON YESTERDAY WHEN MARY BYRD and I stumbled up the hill on our way home from the hospital. We were untidy and stained from the work we had been doing, and so weary we could scarcely put one foot before the other. The firing was slight and I commented on it.

"I wonder why they have stopped so suddenly. I don't like it."

"I expect it's time for tea," Mary Byrd said airily. "Isn't it true that in England everything stops for tea?"

"If only we were in England now!" Then I giggled. "I wonder if the soldiers crook their little fingers when they hold their cups. And do you suppose they're having cucumber sandwiches with their tea?"

"Stop talking about food! If a chicken squawked by right now I'd eat it! Feathers and all!"

I laughed. "Once I would have considered that a disgusting thought."

"Well, maybe I'd pull some of the feathers off," she admitted. "I never knew before what it was to be truly hungry, did you, Rosemary?"

"Never. There may be *something* to eat at our house." Casually I added, "I don't know whether Derek is home or not," and glanced sideways at Mary Byrd. I saw her blush and smiled to myself.

"Well, I'll stop," she said, "but I can't stay long. Mamma goes into a real swivet when the shelling starts and she doesn't know where I am."

We walked across the broad lawn, untended now and full of weeds, and Woof came slowly to meet us. How thin he was! I leaned and stroked him, and together we went into the house. Amanda and Betsy were in the kitchen, Betsy on her mother's lap. Amanda looked up, her face worried.

"What is it?" I asked. "Is Betsy not feeling well?"

"She's so cold, Miss Rosemary. Seems like she can't stop shivering."

"Do you know what's the matter with her?"

"No. I sure wish I did."

I knelt beside the rocking chair and took Betsy's hand in mine. "Where does it hurt, Betsy? What is the trouble, baby, can you tell us?"

Betsy raised dark teary eyes. "I'm so hungry," she murmured, "and I'm so ascared of all the shootin', and my head aches." Burrowing that black curly head in Amanda's shoulder she sobbed quietly.

"I was just about to go get us the milk," her mother said, "and maybe I could get an egg or two. Those neighbors still have a few chickens nobody found yet." She smiled wryly. "They're keeping them in their back parlor so nobody knows. With a dab of milk and an egg I could fix something for the child here. But I can't take her, and I don't like to leave her alone."

"We'll watch her," Mary Byrd said. "You go along, Amanda. We'll take good care of Betsy." She gazed at Amanda in quiet wonder. "I didn't know there was a chicken or a cow left within a hundred miles," she added. "Amanda, you're amazing!"

"Seems I just know some real handy folks," she said rising, and gesturing for me to sit down, she placed Betsy in my lap. "I'll be back soon's I can," she said, gathering up her old cloth bag and going out the kitchen door.

I sat rocking, Betsy huddled in my arms. Mary Byrd sat on the floor beside us, and started to sing very softly. It was some sort of lullaby, and her sweet voice made it a tender, soothing melody. Betsy's eyes began to droop, and after a moment or two I felt her relax in sleep.

"I never heard you sing before," I said quietly. "You have a lovely voice."

"There hasn't been much to sing about lately, sugar. When is it ever going to be over, Rosemary?"

"There was talk about the fourth of July, remember? And that's the day after tomorrow. At least it's quiet now."

Just as I spoke those ill-timed words the guns started again, louder and closer than I had ever heard them. It seemed as if the earth shook with their thunder. Betsy jerked upright in my arms and screamed, and I could not stop her. I cupped my hands over her ears, but it was no help.

"Let's take her down to the basement," I shouted at Mary Byrd. "It may shut out some of the noise."

Mary Byrd nodded, and together we managed to get a hysterical Betsy down the kitchen steps, Woof slinking along beside us. We laid the child on one of the mattresses and I sat beside her and tried to comfort her, but she was beyond hearing me. As the shelling continued, almost paralyzing in its intensity, shriek after shriek came from her, her eyes shifted like those of a frightened horse, her hands clutched at me. Mary Byrd moved close to us, and I don't think either of us knew whether we were huddling together for mutual solace or for protection.

And then a shell crashed through the cellar wall, rolled a few feet toward us, and lay there, round and ugly, hissing. If Betsy had not fainted I am sure I would have. Suddenly I was scanning the walls of the basement frantically.

"The wine racks," I shouted at Mary Byrd. "Behind the wine racks."

She looked at me as if I had gone mad, but when I stood up, leaving Betsy unconscious on the mattress, she rose with me, her eyes on mine. I ran to the wall lined with racks and racks of dusty bottles, pushing against them, pulling at them, muttering to myself, unheard in that continuing racket, glancing over my shoulder at the sinister shell that lay across the basement from us, and I prayed. Oh, how I prayed! And then I felt one tier of shelves give a little under my hand, and as I struggled with it, it slowly came away from the wall, moving on hinges as a door does. Behind it another door opened slowly outward. Woof kept getting under my feet, Mary Byrd was at my shoulder, her blue eyes huge as she stared into the damp, musty-smelling darkness behind that door. When I ran back to the mattress on which Betsy lay, she was beside me, helping me drag child and mattress through the door, into that stygian blackness, helping me shut the door behind us, closing us in. Just as I sank down on the edge of the mattress there came an ear-splitting crash from the other side of the door, followed by the roar of falling wood and plaster, and the sharp sound of shattered glass. I threw myself across Betsy and my head knocked hard against another head, Mary Byrd's, as she did precisely the same thing.

For what seemed an eternity we lay that way, Woof shaking as he huddled close into me, until the noise stopped. I sat up, and when I spoke my voice sounded very loud in the sudden quiet.

"Betsy. Are you all right?"

Her voice was small but clear. "I think so, Miss Romy. But I'm a mite squashed. Why you two ladies pounce on me like that?"

Mary Byrd started to laugh, and after a second I laughed with her. "Squashed!" she said, and went off into another gale. We couldn't stop, until finally, with gasps for breath, she managed to speak. "Where in the name of heaven are we?"

"In a tunnel under the house," I told her.

"Oh." A pause. "Rosemary, *why* is there a tunnel under the house?"

"It's an escape tunnel for slaves."

"Oh." Another pause. "I see. I've heard of them."

There was not a glimmer of light anywhere. The blackness was as thick and heavy as a rug. I could feel Woof trembling against me, but I could not see him. I felt for Betsy's hand and held it tightly in mine, but I could not see her. I groped for Mary Byrd's hand, found it and clasped it. The darkness was absolute.

"I don't think I like this very much," Mary Byrd said. "I wonder what the basement is like. Perhaps we should open the door and look."

"I'll try."

"I'll help."

I stood up and stepped inch by inch toward where I thought the door must be, Mary Byrd clutching my skirt. I felt for the rough wooden surface of the door, and in a step or two, found it.

"It's here," I said, and pushed against the door. It didn't move. "It seems to be stuck."

"Let's push together. One, two, three—*push*!" It was useless. "Maybe if we put our backs against it," Mary Byrd suggested.

Together we leaned our backs against the stubborn door, pushing with all our strength. It did not give an inch. I felt a sudden movement from Mary Byrd and heard her gasp a quick "Oh!"

"What is it?"

"My foot slipped and I twisted my ankle. It's nothing."

"Are you all right?"

"Of course. Let's sit down for a moment and decide what to do next."

But when she tried to take the few steps to the mattress I could hear her inhale sharply, and I knew the ankle must be painful.

"Put your arm across my shoulders and hop," I told her. "I'll hold you up."

With my arm about her waist she hopped, and I helped her settle on a corner of the mattress.

"Is it very bad?" I asked.

"As you would say, Rosemary, don't worry. What do you think we should do now?"

"Be very brave," I answered aloud, and said silently to myself, Be *very* brave, Rosemary! I could feel the cold damp sweat breaking out on my forehead, my face, my arms. It was the old terrifying feeling that I thought familiarity with the cave had banished, but here it was again, worse than I had ever felt it. I clenched my teeth tightly together and tried to slow my breathing. I *had* to keep calm. If Betsy and Mary Byrd even suspected my terror it could affect them, too. My heart was beating so hard I was sure the others could hear it in the silence. In the dark stillness. When Betsy spoke I jumped.

"I've been in here before. Dada showed me this place."

"Your daddy showed you, Betsy?" Mary Byrd asked. "How did he know about it?"

The child's voice held pride. "Dada helped to dig it."

"Your *father*? Hector helped dig this tunnel?"

"Yes, Miss Mary Byrd. It's a great long tunnel, too."

"Does Derek know about it, Rosemary?"

"Yes," I managed, though my voice seemed to squeak.

"I see," Mary Byrd said after a pause. "He never told me."

"I wish there was a light in here," I said. It was almost a whisper.

Betsy moved and was sitting beside me, her hand on my shoulder. I wondered if she could feel me shaking.

"There might be," she said.

"There might be what?"

"A light. A candle maybe. I 'member. When I was here with Dada he showed me little ... shelf things. In the walls. There was a box with candles and matches."

I looked around, straining my eyes, but the darkness was impenetrable. "Where, Betsy? Where were the shelves? Can you remember?" As I spoke I found myself getting to my feet. Anything was better than sitting there shivering.

"They're just sort of stuck on the walls. I don't know where."

"Maybe I can find them."

Mary Byrd's hand grasped my skirt. "Rosemary, sit down! You'll get lost!"

I swallowed hard and tried to sound calm. "If this is a tunnel I can't get very far lost. If I don't find any shelves I'll ... I'll just turn around and come back. Hold Woof's collar. I don't want to trip over him."

Mary Byrd's voice came in a mutter. "I wish somebody would hold *your* collar!"

My knees felt like water, but I forced myself to take a few steps in that solid blackness, stretching out my arms, my fingers brushing along the clay walls. From behind me Betsy spoke.

"The shelves are 'bout at the top of my head," she offered.

"Thank you," I said politely.

This is what it's like to be blind, I thought. Blind

and buried alive. Step by trembling step I moved, fingers trailing along the walls. How far had I come? Not far—I could turn now and in a few steps be back with Betsy and Mary Byrd and Woof. In the dark. No, it was better to go on if there was any chance of light. What an atavistic fear it is, the fear of darkness! I wanted to claw through the walls to light and air. The fingers of my right hand stubbed against rough wood. "Ow!"

"What is it?" Mary Byrd's voice seemed a long way off.

"I think I found a—yes! A shelf! Wait ... there's something ... a box, I think...." My hand, shaking uncontrollably, felt a square outline. I tried to lift it, but it seemed fastened to a wooden shelf projecting from the wall. "I can't see how it opens ... wait ... yes, I can." My blind fingers raised a lid, scrabbled in the box, felt the blessed smooth waxen shape of candles! Matches? Oh, please God, let there be matches! A smaller box, I could feel roughness on the outside. Gently, oh, so gently—I pushed at one end of it. If they should spill I'd never find them! The little drawer of the matchbox opened, inside ... yes ... oh, thank you God! Inside were matches.

"I found them. Candles—and matches! If I can just light one ..."

"I knew they were there," came Betsy's smug voice.

"You are wonderful!" I said, and meant each syllable. With icy cold fingers I took a match from the little box and struck it against the roughness. It sparked and went out. Another. This one broke in my shaking hand. A third. A tiny flame that wavered in my heavy breathing. I closed my mouth tight, held the match carefully until the flame strengthened, took the candle from the box—and lit it! It was like life after death! I had never, in all my life, been so proud of myself. I turned back to where the others must be.

"Look!"

"Just like Mamma tells from the Bible," Betsy remarked. "Let there be light."

"And there was light," Mary Byrd finished, her voice solemn.

Holding the lighted candle, shielding it with my other hand, I moved back. Six shining eyes watched as I approached. I felt exhausted and exhilarated—and almost in control of my fear.

"I 'membered, I 'membered," Betsy crowed, bright-eyed with excitement.

"Where does the tunnel go, Betsy? Can you remember that?"

"I don't know, Miss Romy. Dada and me, we never went all the way. He just showed it to me once, and said he helped dig it. He said it was very long."

I pushed my brain to recall what Hector had said. I could hear his deep voice: "About a mile ..." Could I possibly walk a mile in this clammy place? "I could go along to the end and bring someone back to help us," I said.

"And you'd probably step out right spang in the middle of Yankeedom!" Mary Byrd said flatly. "Don't you move! We're going to sit right here on this mattress until someone gets us out." She stopped suddenly, and when she went on her voice was very small. "Someone *will* get us out, won't they?"

"Of course," I said, trying to sound confident.

How long would it take Amanda to get back? When would Derry come home? It might not be for hours. Would anyone think to look for us here? And if they found us, could they get the door open? There must be piles of rubbish against it . . . I tipped the candle until a little wax dripped onto the floor, and then set the candle in it. My hand felt too weak to hold it any longer. In the small circle of flickering light we all looked at each other.

Mary Byrd reached out one hand and took Betsy's, with her other hand she took mine. Softly she started to sing.

"Row, row, row your boat . . ."

If she could do it, I could. I gritted my teeth against panic, and at the appropriate moment I joined in. A few bars later Betsy's shrill little voice picked up the old round.

"Merrily, merrily, merrily, merrily, life is but a dream." No, like a nightmare, I thought, but we kept singing, over and over, our voices getting louder, until we were shouting the repetitive words at the tops of our lungs.

As I paused for breath I heard what seemed an echo—but the voices were deeper. Male voices. "Row, row, row your boat," they sang determinedly, and from beyond the door came the noise of heavy objects being moved, the crash of broken glass, the scrape of things being pulled across other things. I jumped to my feet and rushed at the door, pounding on it.

"Hello, out there! Let us out! We're stuck in here! Let us out!"

"Just what we're aimin' to do, ma'am," came a deep, cheery voice. "It's a right poor mess out here. You all right?"

"Oh yes! Yes! Who are you?"

"Just three friendly old Southern boys—just you sit tight now."

And then another voice, filled with distress. "Miss Rosemary—is Betsy in there? You got my baby with you?"

"Yes, Amanda," I shouted, "she's here—she's all right!"

Betsy was beside me, beating on the door with her small fist. "Mamma! Mamma! I told Miss Romy 'bout the candles. I 'membered Dada showing me! I did, Mamma, I did!"

"Bless you, Betsy," Amanda said in a voice that wasn't quite steady.

And then the strong masculine voice again. "Stand back from the door, ladies. Stand back."

I took Betsy's hand and moved back to stand beside Mary Byrd, Woof quivering at my knee. With a tremendous wrenching sound the door was pulled open, leaving a space filled with faces. Amanda's, smiling through tears, and three others—men I had seen before—where? Then I recalled. They were men who had begged for the scrapings from Amanda's kitchen bowl.

Dirt-streaked, sweating, haggard, and thin, with torn uniforms and bleeding hands—they were all grinning as they faced us in that almost impassable basement.

I thought my heart would burst open with joy.

I guided Betsy to the opening, noting with relief that whatever ailment she had been suffering earlier had disappeared in (I assumed) the pleasant importance of knowing where light might be found. I kissed her soft cheek as she was lifted straight into her mother's arms.

Then, leaning over Mary Byrd, I placed my arms under hers. "See if you can make it up on your good foot. I'll hold you."

With a tiny wince of pain she pushed herself up until she was standing. The men watched carefully.

"You hurt, ma'am?" one asked. "Why, it's Miss Blair, isn't it? You hurt, Miss Blair?"

"It's nothing. I just twisted my ankle a bit. . . ."

The soldier set one foot into the tunnel, leaned forward and scooped Mary Byrd up as if she had been an armload of feathers. I blew out the candle and stepped out, Woof following closely. Out! I took a deep breath and was almost overcome by the suffocating smell of wine from dozens of broken bottles. The poor Bartletts who owned this house! I hoped they wouldn't think we had drunk all of it.

I turned toward the kitchen stairs. The broken steps were covered with debris.

"How did you get in?" I asked the men.

"The same way the shell did. Through that hole," one

said, and pointed to a wide gap in the wall. "We heard the explosion, and this here lady—" he indicated Amanda, "she was afeared someone might be down here. So we came in, and we heard you-all singin' in there. It sounded real pretty!"

Betsy was boosted through the open space, with Amanda after her, and then one of the men pulled himself through and turned to lift Mary Byrd out, seating her gently on the grass. Then it was my turn, and there was an assist for Woof. Poor Woof! There had been a time when he could have jumped the distance, but not now. I made sure the men climbed out safely and watching them, wondered where they had found the strength to rescue us. Their bodies were close to skeletal from hunger, their faces drawn. And yet they still smiled. When Mary Byrd, in her stained hospital apron, with dirt streaks on her face and cobwebs in her hair, pulled from somewhere a ravishing smile of her own, the men grinned delightedly.

"You're just the sweetest little ol' boys I've had the pleasure of meetin'," she said. "You must give me your names so I can invite you the next time we have a party."

Just at that moment Derek came racing around the side of the house. I had never seen him so white and wild-eyed.

"Tad! Are you all right? Are you hurt?" He put his hands on either side of my face, searching my eyes with his.

"I'm perfectly all right, Derry."

"You're sure?"

I nodded and managed a weak smile. "Don't worry," I said.

Dropping his hands to my shoulders, he looked at me carefully. "What in God's name happened?"

"A shell came into the basement, but I don't think it came in God's name. It hissed at us and then it exploded, but by that time we were safe in the tunnel."

He frowned. "How did you know about the tunnel?"

"You told me, Derry. You and Hector. Behind the wine shelves, you said."

"Oh, yes, of course! And thank heaven you remembered!" He pulled me close against him, holding me tight. I could feel his hands shaking.

"I remembered—but then we couldn't get out. The door was jammed. These men finally got it open."

His arms loosened and he turned, seeing the small crowd around us. He nodded at the three young men. When his eyes found Mary Byrd, a small, dirt-streaked figure sitting on the grass, he took my hand and we went toward her.

"Mary Byrd hurt her ankle," I said.

Mary Byrd's voice was surprisingly cool. "It's nothing. I was clumsy and twisted it."

Releasing my hand, Derry dropped to one knee, lifting back her full skirt. Carefully he pulled off one pink carriage boot, exposing an ankle already badly swollen. His fingers touched it gently, moving around and across.

"I don't think it's broken. We're going into the house and put a cold compress on it. Hold the door, please, Amanda." He lifted Mary Byrd, and then turned to the three men. "And you come in, too. If there's a bottle or two in the cellar that didn't get smashed, we'll be sure they are used properly."

Amanda held the door, Derry strode in with Mary Byrd in his arms, and Betsy and the three soldiers followed. I stood looking around me for a moment, breathing in the fresh early evening air. Supposing I had not known of the tunnel! With a shiver as I realized what might have been, I joined the others, faithful Woof at my heels.

July 3, 1863

ABOUT TEN O'CLOCK THIS MORNING, JULY 3, DERRY and I were in one of the hospitals working, having gone down alone since it was impossible for Mary Byrd to be of use with her injured ankle. I wondered why so few wounded were being brought in, and asked Derek if he knew.

"Let me take a look outside and see if anything is going on," he said. A moment later he was back. "Come and view history at close range, Tad." I followed him out.

From where we stood we had a fair view of much of the defense works that had been built, and along the tops of them were placed many white flags, hanging slack in the windless air.

"They mean surrender, don't they?" I asked.

"They mean at least an armistice on fighting. I imagine the generals are discussing terms."

"That's promising, isn't it? If they are talking together?"

"Very. And Pemberton must accept. He must! These men cannot go on any longer in their half-starved condition."

We went back to work, and I was in a fever of impatience to know what was happening. In the late afternoon Uncle Will arrived and I went to him quickly.

"You always know what is going on, Uncle. Please

tell me! Is the siege over? Has Vicksburg surrendered?"

"As I understand it, Pemberton and General Grant have met somewhere—near a small stunted oak tree, I was told, which has already been chopped into bits for souvenirs—and they are arranging the terms of surrender. Each man wants to do the best he can, of course, but Grant has the upper hand."

"But they have stopped fighting? No more shelling? Or artillery fire? Or anything?"

"Probably not, child. I hope to God not."

As I went about my chores, many of the patients asked what was going on, and I told them as well as I could. There was not a cheer in the vast room. One man turned his head away to hide his tears.

"Poor Vicksburg," he murmured. "She tried so hard."

"It is a gallant city," I said softly, smoothed his hair, and left.

As Derek and I walked home I looked about me. Everywhere were houses and empty shops, either entirely demolished or badly damaged. Scarcely a windowpane remained. In places great trees had fallen, their leaves and splintered limbs stretching over yards of ground. The green hillside was filled with craters where shells had landed. The proud city of Vicksburg had been through a siege, and the scars would show for years.

At the corner of Jackson Street, the street that

sweeps down the length of the bluffs, we heard the all-too-familiar whine of a shell. Derry pushed me tight against the nearest tree, but when the solid thud of the landing came it was a good distance away.

"I thought the shelling was over," I said furiously.

"So did I," said Derry.

As we turned the corner to climb the hill, Mr. Swords, the editor of *The Citizen*, came striding up from the business section of town. His face was strained and weary. Derek greeted him, and added, "We understood the shelling had ceased."

"So did everyone else, Mr. Leigh. Some Yank who couldn't resist one last shot, I suppose."

And just then, from far below us near the river, there came the clear sharp notes of a bugle. My brother's head lifted as he listened.

"That's the truce call, Mr. Swords. There will be no more shelling now. It means peace. Peace, Mr. Swords!"

"It means surrender, Mr. Leigh. Surrender!" He wiped his hands across his face, leaving a smear of ink near his brimming eyes. "If you will excuse me...." And he walked quickly away.

We reached our house and were crossing the front lawn, mutilated now by the shells that had crashed into it, when Hector rounded the side of the house, carrying a spade. He stopped short when he saw us, and then moved forward again, his face long and grave.

"Hector," Derek said. "Something is wrong. Not Amanda? Not Betsy?"

"No, Mr. Derek. They are all right."

"Then?"

"It's Woof, Mr. Derek. He . . . seems like he had to go out of the house just a while ago—just . . . just *out,* Mr. Derek . . ."

"And?"

"And there was that there shell—that last one came over—leastwise everybody's been saying it's the last one . . ."

I couldn't stand it. I grabbed Hector's strong arm and shook it. "What happened, Hector? What *happened*?"

"Part of that shell landed in the backyard, Miss Rosemary. And Woof—well, Woof was right there. Right where it landed."

I turned to run around the house and felt Hector's hand hard on my shoulder. "No, Miss Rosemary! Don't you go back there! I done buried him, but . . . well . . . I haven't got everything cleaned up yet."

I jerked away and raced across the pitted yard and around to the back, and there I stopped—and looked— and retched.

Beside the neat earth mound Hector had dug and filled, the ground was stained a deep crimson-black, and scraps of rusty-brown fur were tangled in the matted grass. Suddenly all the hideous uselessness and cruelty and suffering of war claimed me, and I stood in the late afternoon sun, feeling its warm rays on my face while I wept. Woof, who had been everyone's friend; Woof, who had starved with us; Woof, who had been an innocent victim of man's belligerence. Helpless, devoted, undemanding Woof. I stooped and patted the grave, feeling the soil damp and still cool against my hand.

"Poor Woof," I whispered. "I'm sorry. I'm *so* sorry, Woof!"

And that is what I shall always think of when I remember the end of the siege of Vicksburg.

July 4, 1863

TODAY IS THE FOURTH OF JULY, WHICH I HAVE learned is an important date in American history, and which will become even more important from this day on. I sit writing in such total quiet that my ears ring. The siege of Vicksburg is over. The war between the states goes on, though Derry and Uncle Will say there is no doubt as to the outcome.

"Now that the full length of the Mississippi River is controlled by the Union, the Confederate states must surrender. Otherwise they will be starved out just as Vicksburg has been, trying to oppose a well-fed, well-equipped army. It is impossible to fight under such conditions."

Uncle Will said that, his face grim and serious. "Vicksburg has shown such fortitude and bravery as could barely be expected of any humans," he went on. "It could not continue."

Early this morning I went into the kitchen to find our three savior soldiers awaiting the scrapings from Amanda's bowl. They greeted me as I walked in.

"Good morning, ma'am," one said. "We won't be bothering you much longer."

"I am only glad we could be of some small use," I told him.

"You have kept some of us alive, ma'am. For weeks our rations have been no more than one biscuit and a bit of bacon per day. Rancid bacon! Without this soup

I think we would surely have starved to death. We will never forgive Pemberton!"

"Forgive General Pemberton? I don't understand."

The young man's eyes flashed with anger. "A child would have known better than to shut men up in this cursed trap to starve to death like rats. I have seen my friends carried off—sometimes three or four in one box—dead of starvation! Nothing else, ma'am! No wounds—no disease—just starvation! Starved to death because we had a fool for a general!"

"Don't you think you are too hard on him? He must have suffered, too."

"Hah!" It was a harsh, cold sound. "Some people may make excuses for him, but we'll curse him to our dying day." I could see tears suddenly fill his eyes, and he wiped his hand across his face in embarrassment before he spoke again. "But it's over now here in Vicksburg. You'll be seeing the blue-coats right soon, I imagine."

"So quickly?"

"They have no reason to wait. Old Granny Pemberton and General Grant will meet this afternoon to sign the official surrender papers, but that is just a formality. The siege of Vicksburg is over. And again, ma'am, blessings on you!"

He held out his hand and I took it, and then the thin hands of the other two. I felt very close to them.

Just then Derek called me to come up to the highest gallery. "And bring Amanda and Betsy. I am going to fetch Mary Byrd. She must see this."

My brother dashed out the door, not even pausing to

put on his jacket. I couldn't blame him, the air was swelteringly hot. As Amanda and Betsy and I went up the beautiful stairs and out onto the balcony my hand reached automatically for Woof's rough head, and my throat choked as I remembered.

Far below us we could see the Vicksburg garrison marching out, flags flying, bands playing, forming a proud straight line, stacking their arms on the ground and marching back again. From bastion after bastion they came, and from the Union troops who watched there was utter quiet. No derisive words, no cheers of victory, just a respectful silence.

Presently a blue-coated soldier sauntered along, gazing about him with curiosity. Two or three more followed, looking like tourists in a strange city. A moment later there was a shout from the street and everyone was pointing to the courthouse, high on the crest of the topmost hill. As we watched, the Union flag, with its brilliant stars and stripes, rose slowly to the top of the pole where the breeze caught it and it sprang out like a live thing. There was a long, low "Aaaaah!" from the crowd. Whether it came from grief or relief I did not know.

It was some time before Derek came back, and he was alone.

"Where's Mary Byrd?" I asked.

"She chose not to come."

"But why?"

His face tightened. "I don't want to talk about it, Tad."

I hesitated. I don't like to pry, but my brother looked so miserable ... "Derek. Please tell me."

He turned his face away, looking out at the mass of gray and blue uniforms. His voice was so quiet I could barely hear him. "She told me she had learned that I knew of the tunnel under this house, that Hector had helped to dig it. To her mind that knowledge makes me a traitor to the Southern cause."

"Oh, Derry!" I remembered Betsy's words in the tunnel, her pride in her father. I remembered saying that Derry had known of it. "What did you say?"

His chin went up. "More than I should have. I didn't mention Uncle Will, of course, nor the Bartletts—though she must know they were involved—but I told her I had helped runaway slaves in whatever small way I could and that I felt no guilt. I told her that I could never believe slavery was right, that I could never believe it was right to own humans. Never!"

"And so?"

"And so she politely requested me to leave, and I did."

"But she loves you, Derek! I know she does!"

"Not enough to give up her principles. I must respect her for that."

I laid my hand on his where it rested on the iron grillwork of the gallery. There was nothing more I could say. In silence we stood, watching the crowd below us.

It must have been almost noon when there seemed to be a rush toward the riverbank. Derry pointed.

"See there, Tad. The ships coming round the bend."

"What are they?"

"Supply boats from the north. Vicksburg has surrendered. Its people need no longer starve."

I stared as a small fleet of transports swept like proud dowagers around the curve of the river, anchoring where only two days before the Confederate batteries had waited for their prey. Now we could make out rope lines and then gangplanks being thrown from ship to shore, and crates being landed. That was when Hector came almost running across the lawn.

"You best come right away, Mr. Derek," he shouted up at us. "There's coffee and sugar and flour on those ships—*white* flour! Other things, too. Hurry!"

"I'm coming, Hector. Wait for me."

A moment or two later we saw him join Hector in the crowd that was flowing down the hill.

Amanda and Betsy and I stayed on the gallery in the hot July sun, and Derry's words kept going round and round in my head. "A traitor to the Southern cause." We watched as the people of Vicksburg trudged back uphill, their arms filled with food from the ships. One man chomped on an apple, the juice running over his chin. He even ate the core. Could these people be called traitors? Accepting aid from their Northern enemies? Some pushed barrows loaded with canned goods, others carried sacks of flour or sugar on their shoulders. Did they feel that it demeaned them, this enthusiastic grasping at what they had been denied? Or was hunger so powerful a force that it erased such lesser concerns as moral right and wrong? I could not believe that in all Vicksburg there was one citizen who would refuse this food. Not even Mary Byrd.

When Derek and Hector returned they carried more supplies than we had seen in months. Amanda's dark, thin face creased in a smile.

"Come along, Betsy child," she said. "Let's us get a fire going and feed this family proper!"

As Betsy scampered ahead her mother paused and touched my arm. "I couldn't help but hear some of what Mr. Derek said. Are you weeping in your heart, Miss Rosemary?"

"Yes, for Derry. But I'm angry! How can Mary Byrd have such useless stiff-necked pride?"

"It's that stiff-necked pride that has held Vicksburg together through these long months. I can't call it useless."

"But they love each other, Amanda! It's as plain as . . . as—doesn't love mean anything?"

"It means most everything. But there's more than one kind of love. There's love of one's own people, too. Sometimes we have to choose." And then she was gone.

After leaving his precious load of foodstuffs in the kitchen, Derry came back out on the gallery.

"Come downstairs and walk out to the street with me, Tad. There's something we must see."

"What's that?" I asked, following him.

"The Union army of occupation. This is a part of American history, my little Britisher. We're fortunate to see it."

As we walked across the front lawn, watching our

step because of the shell holes, I said impulsively, "I wonder whether Mary Byrd is watching."

"I doubt it," said Derek.

At the edge of the grass, where the roadway went by, we stood, surrounded by other viewers. And what a sight it was! The long blue column was led by officers on sleek, groomed horses, their trappings polished and gleaming. The riders' uniforms were brushed and clean, their heads were high, their eyes clear and alert. They looked well fed and cared for, both horses and men, and as proud as I was of them, my heart ached to see the sad comparison between these troops and the weak, shabby, undernourished men in gray who looked on in silence.

Behind the horses came an endless line of marching men, healthy, straight-backed, and serious. No face wore the smirk of triumph. They seemed to exude a quiet confidence, these young conquerors, and the steady dust-raising beat of their feet brought a sense of order.

As we watched, unspeaking, a Union soldier turned his head as he neared us, and his hand jerked in a sharp salute. I could not believe it! Jeff! Though they all looked the same, I *knew* it was Jeff! I lifted my hand and waved. He passed close by us, his eyes—how deep a brown they were!—directly on mine. His voice reached me clearly.

"May I stop in to see you later?"

"Of course!"

"Here?" he asked. His eyebrows lifted comically as he glanced at our "mansion."

"Yes," I called as he moved past me. "Here."

He nodded quickly, gave another salute, and marched away. My eyes followed until he was out of sight. When I turned back Derek was watching me quizzically.

"Jeff Howard, hmm?"

"Yes."

He smiled. "You're blushing."

"I *never* blush!"

"Then it must be a touch of the sun. Well, perhaps between us we lose one and gain one in the same day."

I looked up at him quickly. "Don't say that, Derry. Don't say it! Maybe Mary Byrd just needs a little time—to think. To get used to the idea."

"She may have all the time she wants. But I am afraid it goes deeper than that. Come along. There should be real food ready for us about now."

"Derry! Don't you *care?*"

His eyes were very sober as they met mine. "I care more than you can possibly imagine, Tad. Now come along."

July 4, 1863

EVENING

I CAN'T REMEMBER WHAT WE HAD FOR OUR EVENING meal. Very likely it was something much more palatable than we had eaten for months, but all I could think of was seeing Jeff again. I worried about my shabby old clothes, the lack of shoes—I was in quite a state when the doorbell finally rang.

Derry answered the door. "Jeff!" I heard him say. "Welcome back. Come in. Rosemary has been eager to see you."

Blast Derek! But it didn't matter.

"I hoped she would be," said Jeff, and strode into the room. His solemn face greeted me, breaking immediately into a wide smile.

"Rosemary!" He came forward quickly, took my two hands in his, and leaning forward, kissed my cheek. "How I have missed you!"

I clenched the hands holding mine. "And I you," I said, surprised to find how true it was.

Derry looked at us, seemed about to sit down in his favorite chair, changed his mind, cleared his throat, and announced, "If you two will excuse me, I believe I'll take a walk."

"Very well," I said, barely hearing him.

"It's a pleasant night," said Jeff.

"Good," said Derek. He gave us another long look, and departed.

It was a beautiful evening. We talked and talked. Jeff told me of the constant Union advance into the South: "I have been almost across the river from you for weeks. You can't think how much I wanted to dive in and swim to the Vicksburg side."

I told him of the lack of food—the lack of everything. "But there were transport ships this afternoon. They brought all sorts of things we have been missing."

And then quite suddenly we were no longer talking about the siege. Jeff sat beside me on the sofa, his hands holding mine, his eyes seeming to see deep into me.

"Rosemary, you haven't changed, have you?"

"I must have. In some ways I must have."

"But you are still Rosemary Leigh, the very beautiful English girl who could not say where her heart belonged in this war. The girl whose beliefs were with the North, and whose affections were with the South. The stormy girl who accused me of coming back to fight the friends I had made in Vicksburg. I have not fired one shot at Vicksburg, Rosemary, and very few at anyplace else. I am a cartographer—a mapmaker. I took up a pen instead of a gun."

I looked at him squarely. "I am glad, Jeff. Oh, I am so glad!"

"I hoped you would be. I hoped you would let me tell you. I was afraid you might not want to see me."

"Jeff, I said dreadful things to you the last time we met. It was unforgivable...."

He laid a finger across my lips. "Hush. I'm glad you

said them. If I had meant nothing to you, you would not have bothered." He grinned. "At least that is how I have comforted myself. If it isn't true, don't tell me. Tell me instead what you plan to do when this is all over."

"Do? I don't really know. I suppose we will have to leave this house—the owner will be coming back ... we haven't talked much about the future. What are *your* plans?"

"I'm still in the Union Army, of course, and I don't know when I'll be released. Then I hope to really study mapmaking. It's fascinating. And I want to visit England, especially London, and I may decide to stay and finish school there. Will you be going back?"

"I don't know. The house in London where we grew up belongs to Derry now, but the law business with Uncle Will is here. And then—I was so sure he was going to marry Mary Byrd, but now that's in a bit of a jumble, and he's so unhappy, and I don't know how to help him, and—oh, I'm so glad to see you again!" I reached out and took both his hands. His fingers were warm and strong on mine.

"Is there anything I can do? Do you want to talk about the jumbled bit?"

"I don't know what to say. I'm only now beginning to learn how—oh, Jeff, Northerners and Southerners, in America, see some things so differently! It's no one's fault—people generally grow up thinking and believing as their parents and grandparents did. About big things, I mean. Little things change with the generations, I suppose, but the big things like—oh, what's right and what's wrong, for example ... I shouldn't be saying all this!"

"Don't tell me anything you don't want to, Rosemary. In any case, I think I can guess the cause of part of your confusion. Mary Byrd is very Southern. Derek thinks like a Northerner. And the issue was slavery."

I stared at him. "How did you know?"

"At the time I first met you I was staying with your uncle, William Stafford. Remember? He and I talked a lot together. He told me of his rather minor—his word, not mine—help to escaping slaves."

"He told you about that?"

"Yes. And other things, such as the fact that Derek had started working with him—not a great deal, but if someone like Mary Byrd learned of it ..."

"You've known all that and never ... you're incredible!"

He grinned his engaging grin. "And you're beautiful. Just for a moment, think about yourself—and me. Whatever your plans may be, be sure to include me in them. Because I intend to be a part of your life—a large part—and you had best get used to the idea. Will you?"

I felt blissfully warm and comfortable. "Yes, Jeff. I will. I most certainly will!"

Not long after that he rose. "I must get back to quarters. I've overstayed my pass as it is."

"Just one more minute, Jeff, there is something I have to know. Those cards you sent me—I can see why

you are an excellent . . . cartographer, is it?—the draw-
ings are so perfect and so delicate! But how did you get
those cards to me? No mail was coming into Vicksburg."

"You would be amazed at the comings and goings
there were between the Confederate and Union armies.
We even had *The Citizen* delivered daily across the
river. It wasn't hard to find a Johnny Reb who would
deliver an envelope in exchange for half a loaf of
bread."

"I suppose not. They have suffered so! They have
starved. Quite literally! They would have done murder
for half a loaf of bread."

"Hush, girl. Hush. It is over now. The transports
will be coming in regularly with supplies."

"But for so many they come too late."

"There has been—and will be—tragedy on both
sides, Rosemary. That is what war brings. But for us
the important thing to remember is that you are here,
and I am here, and we have a future. Hold on to that."

And then he very gently put both arms around me
and kissed me thoroughly on the lips. I had never
guessed how wonderful that could be! I wished it
wouldn't stop, but it did.

"Good night, girl. Sleep well," he said, and was gone
into the quiet night.

I stood for a moment, my hand on the doorknob, and
fancied it still warm from his touch. I hugged myself,
feeling his arms around me, and my lips still tingled
from his kiss. It was all so natural, so right. The night
was still, I felt very safe, and so happy.

* * *

Taking a candle I started for the kitchen to be sure the fire was out for the night and that the back door was locked. The end of the siege did not make the city secure. Hector had come tonight to take Amanda and Betsy back to their home and had said there were Southern soldiers drifting into Vicksburg from outlying areas, hoping for food.

"Some of them are a mite nasty, Miss Rosemary. An empty belly can make a man powerful mean. Just you be careful."

The kitchen door was securely closed. As I checked it I heard a low whimpering sound from outside. An animal? A child? Could it be Betsy, returned for some reason? I opened the door a crack.

"Betsy?" I whispered. "Is that you?"

But it was not Betsy's voice that answered. "Let me in, Rosemary. Let me in! Let me in!"

I threw the door wide. "Ben!"

He slid around the door into the house, closed the door, and dropped the heavy hook into its hasp. Leaning against the wall, he hid his face in his hands.

"I thought you'd never come," he mumbled. "I've been waiting—and waiting—someone was here. Was he looking for me, Rosemary? Did you tell him where I was?"

"Ben! No one was looking for you—what is the trouble? Come in. Here, sit down here." I took his arm and led him, stumbling, to Amanda's rocking chair, and thrust him gently into it. He buried his face in his hands again, and seemed to weep.

"It's too quiet here, Rosemary. I don't like it when everything is so quiet. Is everyone dead? Is that why everything is so quiet?"

I looked at him closely. His torn uniform, his skin, his hair were filthy. His bones stood out as if he were a skeleton, the skin pulled tight. He smelled of sweat and vomit and fear.

"Are you hungry, Ben?"

"I can't eat anything. It won't stay down."

"When did you eat last?" As I spoke I moved to the stove. A pan of cooled coffee stood there, and using the poker I prodded at the embers that remained, adding a few sticks of wood that flared up quickly.

"I don't know. I don't recall. It doesn't matter."

I went to the larder, cut a slice of white bread from the loaf Amanda had baked that afternoon, and spread it with the last of a jar of grape preserves.

"Where have you been, Ben?"

"In a cave. I found a cave. There was no one in it."

"How long were you in the cave?"

"I don't know. Some days. A long time. What does it matter? But it got too quiet. I'm afraid of the quiet."

"The siege of Vicksburg is over, Ben. That's why it's quiet. Here, drink some coffee. It is hot. It will be good for you. And here's bread—white bread, Ben. Have a bite."

He twisted away from me. "I don't want any. Take it away."

"Ben, you must eat!"

"I can't! I can't! I can't! Just the smell of it . . ."

And suddenly he retched, an empty, terrible retching, with only a little bile escaping from his mouth. I held his straining head and wiped his face with my handkerchief. And then the most welcome sound in the world, Derry's voice from the front of the house.

"Tad? Where are you?"

"In the kitchen. Please come!"

He stopped in the doorway. "What's the matter? Who is—? Ben!"

"He's frightfully ill. He can't eat—he's been hiding in a cave, heaven knows how long—oh, I'm so glad you're home!"

Derek dropped to one knee beside the rocking chair and laid his hand on Ben's forehead, then against his cheek.

"He's cold, Tad. Awfully cold." He raised his voice. "Ben. What is it, old man? What can we do for you?"

Ben's head rested against the back of the rocker, eyes closed. When he spoke his voice was no more than a thread of sound. "Let me sleep. I want to sleep in your basement. I felt safer there. Everything is too quiet. It frightens me when everything is so quiet. Why aren't there guns?"

"The war in Vicksburg is over, Ben. No more guns in Vicksburg."

"Don't believe it. They're just waiting. They're going to kill us all. Every one of us. Everyone in Vicksburg. Dead! Dead! Dead!"

"The basement is impossible," Derry said to me. "We'll put him in my bed. He can sleep there."

"He can barely walk. I'll help you. What's the matter with him?"

"Shock. Fatigue. Starvation. Who can say?"

One on each side of Ben, we pulled his arms across our shoulders and step by laborious step we walked him into Derry's room. Once he was on the bed we stripped him of as much clothing as we could. How thin he was! His flesh barely covered his bones. I fetched an extra blanket and covered him tightly. He was so cold! We stood looking down at him, the young man who had been so lighthearted, so proud of his uniform, teasing and joking and friendly, and, as if he read my thoughts, Derry said softly, "That's what war does, Tad. You should not have to see these things." He turned away and walked to a window, gazing out into darkness. "I should never have brought you back to America with me. I should have stayed with you, in London. I've thought that a hundred times during these past months."

I looked at his handsome, dark head, his broad shoulders, his hands clasped behind his back. I spoke softly.

"And what would you have done in London, Derry? You had made a life here."

"I could have become a doctor, perhaps. Or a barrister." He turned back to me, his face serious. "And certainly looked out for you better than I have been able to do here in Vicksburg."

"And denied me the chance to learn more about the world? About America? About people? People with strong beliefs, who are willing to fight for them? I think I would be a lesser person now, if that had happened."

He came back to me, putting one arm across my shoulders and walking with me toward the door.

"But a happier one," he said. "I am constantly awed by your strength, little sister. I have enormous respect for you. Now go to bed. I will stay here with Ben."

I reached up and kissed his cheek. "Try to sleep," I said, and went to my own room.

July 5, 1863

BEN NEVER WOKE THE NEXT MORNING. NOT EVER.
Derry fetched a doctor who pronounced it "death from
natural causes," adding, "if you can call fear and starvation natural."

Since neither of us knew how to reach Ben's family, it
seemed we must take the sad news to the Blairs. I told
Derek I would go and although he demurred he finally
agreed it might be wiser.

It seemed strange to walk the streets without listening for the whine of a shell. Already there were both
men and women at work, gathering boards into piles
and removing nails from those that might be salvage-
able, sweeping streets and walks clear of debris, sawing
broken tree branches into firewood, doing what they
could to restore their city. They made me think of ants,
scurrying to rebuild a hill that had been carelessly
trodden on.

Mr. Blair met me in the wide entrance hall. He had
been shoveling a pile of broken plaster into a barrel.
Ruefully he indicated a section of the ornate ceiling
that had come down.

"And that was just from vibration," he said, setting
the shovel against the wall. "We were not hit, as you
were. I assume you want to see Mary Byrd."

"I came to bring you some sad news. Ben, your

nephew, died last night. At our house. We did not know whom else to tell. I am so sorry!"

For a long moment he stood staring at me. "Ben?" he repeated. I nodded. Then, very slowly, he sat down on one of the stairs, dropping his head into his hands.

"How did he die?" he asked presently. "He had not been wounded again, had he?"

"No. Derek called a doctor who said it was from—from fear and starvation."

After a moment Mr. Blair started to speak, slowly and quietly. "Poor Ben. He should never have had to be a soldier. Ben liked parties, and good times. He would have been happy as a successful plantation owner, hiring a foreman to take care of things and just enjoying himself. But the only way of life we knew is gone. It will never come back—not as it was. Not as good as it was." He lifted his head and smiled at me, a sad smile. "A way of life you could never understand, Rosemary. But it was all we ever knew." He got to his feet stiffly. "I will see to things for Ben. If he may stay—wherever he is just for a little . . ."

"He is in my brother's bed. We put him there last night. Derek is with him."

"Thank you. I am glad he was not alone. I will have him moved directly." He put his hand on my shoulder. "Go up and see Mary Byrd. She has not come out of her room since yesterday. She won't talk to her mother or me. Is it trouble with your brother, Rosemary?"

"Yes, I think so." I paused and then added, "He hoped to marry her, Mr. Blair."

He looked straight at me. "Did he now! You can't think how much Mrs. Blair and I hoped for that, too. We thought perhaps he might take her back to England with him—get her away from all that has changed here. And now there's disagreement?"

"I am afraid so. They have—different points of view, you know."

"Can you tell me?"

"I don't think so. It's just—different points of view."

He sighed heavily. Poor man! So many things to worry him! "Go up and see her. Perhaps she will talk to you. And tell her about Ben."

"I am not sure she wants to see me."

"Please try. You and she have been so close. Just try."

"Very well." I went up the familiar staircase and tapped on Mary Byrd's door. "It's Rosemary. May I come in?"

After a moment the door was opened and Mary Byrd turned away from it and walked slowly back to a chair by the window. I closed the door behind me, moved across to her unmade bed, and sat on the edge of it. I told her about Ben.

She still did not look at me. "Poor Ben," she whispered. "He was one of my favorite people. I'm glad you were with him. I think he loved you, Rosemary."

I sat silently, looking at her. She was still in a shabby frock she must have slept in—if she had slept at all. Her beautiful hair was a tangle, her eyes were red from weeping, and there were deep shadows below them. I took her hairbrush from her dresser and started to work on the matted golden curls. At first she stiffened and a hand went up in protest. Then she closed her eyes and leaned back.

"That feels nice. I suppose I am a mess."

"You certainly are."

"Did—did Derek come with you?"

"No. Would you have seen him if he had?"

"No," she said softly. "We have nothing to say to each other."

"He had a great deal to say to you, Mary Byrd. He wanted to marry you."

"Did he tell you so?"

"Yes, he told me. I was so happy."

"I was happy, too, just knowing that he loved me. I would have said yes to him—just a short time ago. But not now."

I continued brushing her hair for a few moments in silence. Then I washed her face with water from the pitcher, sprinkled a few drops of precious toilet water on my hand, and smoothed it across the back of her neck. Standing behind her, my hands on her shoulders, I spoke again.

"Mary Byrd, I know that you and Derek are from different cultures, that you were each raised with different concepts of how your worlds should be. But . . ."

She interrupted. "There are no 'buts.' You have said it all. We are from different cultures. And people rarely change."

"Have you thought how your world has changed? And it will never be the same again. How will you live in it?"

"I don't know. But I will—somehow. I must."

"Derek loves you, Mary Byrd."

"I know he does," she whispered. "And I love him. But it's no use, Rosemary. You had better go now."

I knew there was nothing more I could say. I leaned down, gently kissed her cheek, left the room and the house.

That afternoon four men arrived with a coffin. Derry and I stood by while Ben was laid in it and carried away.

Late July 1863

For the last several weeks life has been busy. Derry and Hector helped Uncle Will put the law office back into functioning order, and Amanda and I moved the bedding out of the cellar and into the rooms we had previously slept in.

The Union transports came almost daily for a while, bringing lumber and nails and window glass and medicines and many of the comforts and necessities we had been without. Shops have begun to reopen, streets have been cleared of debris, the caves are being flattened, and *The Citizen* now appears on proper newsprint. Life in Vicksburg, if by no means normal, is far better than it has been for months.

I still went to the hospitals for part of each day, until the last patients were well enough to be discharged, and Derry joined me when he could. Mary Byrd never came. I did not see her at all.

A few days ago Jeff was ordered to leave with his regiment for Tennessee, and we said goodbye. I had seen him often, and each time we were together the bond between us became stronger. Now that we are apart I yearn to have his arms about me and his kisses on my lips. Someday, we promised each other. Someday! He still talked of going to England and perhaps studying in London, and that made it easier for me to accept Derek's decision that it was time he and I returned there.

"Not necessarily forever, Tad, although it may work out that way. But I must see how our house is faring since the tenants left it, and there are business and financial things that should be taken care of. There's something else, too, that I haven't mentioned to you. I am considering seriously the idea of entering medical school. Does that astonish you?"

I was silent for a moment, and then said, "Not entirely. I have seen how much you learned from Papa, and how capable you were in the hospitals here. I think you will make a superb doctor!"

"London has some of the best medical schools," he said, "and teaching hospitals, too."

"Uncle Will can manage all right without you?"

"Perfectly. There are many young lawyers who would be overjoyed to take my place. I have talked with him about all this, and he feels you and I should go home, at least for a while. We can always come back if we want to."

"There's not much to come back to, is there?" I said.

"Not without Mary Byrd, there isn't."

It was hard for me to tell Amanda, and there were tears in her eyes as well as in mine.

"We've been through a lot together, Miss Rosemary, but it's right that you go home. This has been a sad place for you. Betsy and I—we'll surely miss you."

"I am going to miss both of you—so very much! And Hector, too. Without you I think we would never have managed these last dreadful months."

That afternoon I went into the slowly reviving shopping streets and found a bookshop that had writing and penmanship books. I bought one of each for Betsy. When I gave them to her I told her I wanted her to write to me, and that these were to help her. "Your mother will help you learn, and you will send me letters often. Please?"

She gave me a teary smile and nodded. "And maybe someday I'll come there to see you, Miss Romy. Is London as far as Liberia?"

"I expect it is, or very close. I hope you *do* come!"

After the sorting of old clothes, the purchase of a few new ones, the cleaning of the house, the decisions on which of our possessions to take and which to get rid of, there was one last thing I had to do. The day before we were to leave I went to the Blairs' house and knocked firmly on the door. Mary Byrd herself opened it, wearing a large white apron. She was paler and thinner, but her pleasure at seeing me was immediately evident.

"Rosemary! Oh, come in! I have missed you so."

"I wasn't sure you would want to see me." I stepped into the hall as she closed the door behind me.

"I have longed to see you, but I didn't know how you felt. Come into the kitchen with me. I am trying to learn to cook—we have had to let most of the servants go. Daddy lost a great deal of money, you know, when the plantation was ruined. . . ." She stopped suddenly in the doorway to the kitchen and turned to me. "I rattle on as I always did, don't I? I expect it's because I'm embarrassed. I've wanted so much to see you, and now I don't know what to say."

In the kitchen I placed one straight chair close by another. "Sit down," I said. "We'll talk."

"I'm trying to learn to make biscuits."

"I'll show you how to make biscuits in a few minutes. Amanda taught me. Sit down." Her eyes on my face, she sat, and I took one of her hands in both of mine. "Derry and I are leaving tomorrow for London."

I could feel her hand jerk. "For long?"

"I don't know. Perhaps forever."

"Oh no!" She looked away and the blue eyes were bright with tears. "Not you, too. Everything is gone. My city, my faith in my beliefs, my pretty ... illusions—now you and Derek."

"Your mother and father hoped you would marry Derry."

"I know. They told me. But he never asked me."

"If he had, you would have said no. You wouldn't even see him."

"I couldn't." She drew her hand from mine and brushed at the tears. "Derek and I have never talked about serious things." She gave me a watery smile. "You know how I am, sugar, I just chatter on and try to say the things people want to hear. It's what everyone expects of Southern girls. We—Derek and I—we never discussed the future. I knew he ... he cared for me, and I have loved him so much for such a long time—well, I suppose I just reckoned we'd be married someday, and live here in Vicksburg, and have a pretty house, and a lot of parties, and some babies ... then I found there were differences in the ways we thought.

Thought about things that were important to each of us. Like his helping runaways to escape. It seemed right to him, but to me it was—it was shocking! I felt he was deliberately working against that lovely world I had always known. But now . . ."

She stopped. With one hand she lifted a corner of the apron and wiped her eyes.

"Now?" I prompted.

She looked away from me. Her voice was very small. "Now I know that lovely world—the one I believed in—was a dream world. Not the real one. It was filled with pleasure and comfort, with pretty clothes—with everything I wanted. Or thought I wanted. I just expected it would always be like that." She sighed. "My daddy says it will never be the same again."

"Perhaps it will be better," I said.

She shrugged lightly. "Perhaps."

"Do you still consider what Derry did to be wrong? And Mr. Bartlett? And our Uncle William?"

She was quiet for a moment, as if searching for a truthful answer. Then her chin lifted. "It was wrong because it was against the law. But it was right, too, because we should not withhold help when we can give it." She looked straight at me. "You see, Rosemary, I never knew those slaves needed help. They were just— there. Had always been. And I thought they *wanted* to be."

I sat back in my chair, looking at her closely. This was a different Mary Byrd from the one I had thought I knew. "What has changed you?" I asked.

She got up and moved restlessly around the kitchen, her fingers touching things as she passed, as if for reassurance in the stability of homely objects.

"I reckon maybe I've grown up a little," she said. "My poor daddy—he should have had a son, not a flutterhead like me. Since Champion Hill was attacked he keeps wanting to talk about it. He never talked to me about serious things before—I don't know what to say to him. He told me it wasn't the Yankees who set fire to our house, it was the slaves of another planter. They were running away. When the Union troops got close those slaves killed their master—I knew him, Rosemary! I knew him! Then they set fire to his buildings and rioted through the countryside, doing as much terrible damage as they could. Daddy told me their owner was known for his cruelty to his people—he told me of punishments that made me sick to hear. And he told me how many such planters there were, and what their slaves endured. My daddy never lies, Rosemary. Never! And so I began to see what a fairy tale I had lived in. Everything isn't always rosy and happy the way I thought it was—thought it would always be." She sniffed loudly, using the hem of the apron again.

"What will your father do now, Mary Byrd?"

She looked at me, the beautiful eyes red-rimmed. "I'm so proud of him!" Moving slowly she came back to the kitchen table, perching on the edge of it. "My daddy's a fighter! You see, our house wasn't totally burned—our own people came back as soon as the rioters went away. They—our people—they managed to

save most of the main house and some of the outbuild-
ings. Now Daddy thinks he can borrow enough money
on what's left of the place to let him hire some of his
sla—, I mean field-hands, back. He plans to sell this
house and move out to Champion Hill with Mamma
and run the place himself."

"And you?"

"I guess I'll go with them." She gave me a lopsided
smile. "It was so nice back in that fairy-tale life. It's
too bad real life isn't like that. But what's a fairy tale
without a prince?" Suddenly she reached forward and
grasped my hand. "Oh, Rosemary, what will I do without you both? The only thing in my whole world that
hasn't changed is my love for Derek. And for you."

I stood up and hugged her. "That may be all you'll
need," I said. "Now I'll teach you how to make biscuits."

Derek was home when I got there, adding a few items
to an open trunk. With no warning I said, "I have just
come from seeing Mary Byrd."

His hands stopped moving. Then he turned his head
and looked at me. "And?"

"I will quote her directly, Derry. She said that the
only thing in her world that hadn't changed was her
love for you."

He straightened. "She actually said that?"

"Precisely that."

He grabbed his jacket from the back of a chair and
pulled it on. I heard his steps, almost running, cross

the rooms to the front door, and then the door slamming behind him.

It was dinnertime when Derry returned. I was in the kitchen with Amanda and Betsy. He stopped in the doorway, looked at us all, smiled broadly and said, "Amanda, do you think you could make a wedding cake by tomorrow morning?"

Amanda turned slowly, gazed at him, and then laughed joyously. "Mr. Derek, I can make you the finest cake anyone ever tasted!" Going to him, she laid her hands on either side of his face. "The Lord love you both!" she said.

Right after dinner Derry rushed off again. "I must see Uncle Will and ask him to be my best man. Oh, I forgot to tell you, Tad. Mary Byrd says of course you will be her maid of honor."

"Of course I will! Now go!"

Although Derry and I talked late into the night, I never heard just what took place between him and Mary Byrd that afternoon. We conversed in disjointed fragments.

"What made you go to see her today?" Derry asked.

"I couldn't have left without trying to. Not possibly."

Derry smiled. "Thank God for that! She's fretting because she has no decent clothes. When we get to New Orleans you must go with her to find things. And then, when we reach London, she can go wild in the shops. I want to buy her every beautiful thing there is!"

"How did Mr. and Mrs. Blair accept the news?"

"They were delighted! Did you know they had been hoping Mary Byrd and I would marry?"

"Yes, I knew that. Mr. Blair told me the day Ben died."

"But you never told *me*!"

"It would have done no good then. Remember I once said perhaps she needed time to think?"

My brother reached out and took my hand. "Women are wonderful creatures!" he said.

I'm sure I had a smug smile on my face when I fell asleep.

The End of July 1863

I AM WRITING THIS AS I SIT ON THE DECK OF THE RIVER-boat. Mary Byrd and Derry stand close together at the rail, their hands locked, watching the Mississippi roll by. We can no longer see those who came to wave us off: the Blairs, Uncle Will, and Amanda and Betsy and Hector, his shirt snowy white against his dark face. Even the flag whipping from the top of the courthouse has become invisible. Now we are gliding by plantations, the burned fields empty of men and crops.

Mary Byrd and Derry were married this morning, just a few hours before we boarded the riverboat. The house had been filled with every available flower. Mary Byrd looked beautiful and ethereal, wearing a white lace shawl of her mother's over her shining hair, clasping a white prayer book in shaking hands. When Amanda and Betsy delivered the wedding cake—a confection such as I had never thought to see again—Mary Byrd asked them to stay for the ceremony. Hector arrived, driving Uncle Will, and he, too, was a guest. The minister was a longtime friend of the Blairs', and the ring Derek slipped on his bride's finger had been our mother's.

As I listened to the beautiful solemn words of the marriage service, I thought of the last time I had seen Jeff. I had told him the silly poem Derry used to tease me with:

"Rosemary Monica Stafford Leigh
Lived at the top of a tamarack tree.
The wind blew strong and the wind blew free
And toppled that towering tamarack tree
With Rosemary Monica Stafford Leigh,
Who fell kerplop and bloodied her knee."

Jeff had smiled, and then drew a bit of paper from his pocket and started to write. After a moment he handed it to me and I read,

" 'Now I'm back on my feet,' said Miss Rosemary
Leigh,
'I've lived through a siege to help others be free.
There's no way to say what the next years may
be,
But I'll spend them with Jeff, who promises me
He won't let me fall from the tamarack tree.' "

There were happy tears in my eyes when I kissed him.

So now we are embarked on the slow journey to London. We will spend a few days in New Orleans, waiting for the ship that will take us across the Atlantic and buying some clothes for Mary Byrd. I look at the towns as we pass them. We will come to Natchez soon, and I think of Prince, who spent fifty years of his life there, in slavery. How he must have suffered! People are suffering still, for the war goes on, but ahead of us the way is clear. New Orleans, and then the wide clean ocean, and then London. And Jeff!

Bibliography

ALFORD, TERRY. *Prince Among Slaves*. New York: Harcourt Brace Jovanovich, 1977.

ANDREWS, WAYNE. *Pride of the South*. New York: Atheneum, 1979.

BLOCKSON, CHARLES L. "The Underground Railroad." *National Geographic* (July 1984).

BUTLER, PIERCE. *The Unhurried Years*. Baton Rouge: Louisiana State University Press, 1948.

CARTER, SAMUEL, III. *The Final Fortress*. New York: St. Martin's Press, 1980.

EWING ELIZABETH. *Dress and Undress*. New York: Drama Book Specialists, 1978.

GRANT, GENERAL U. S. "The Siege of Vicksburg." *The Century Illustrated Monthly Magazine,* vol. 8 (May–October 1885).

PAYNE, BLANCHE. *History of Costume*. New York: Harper & Row, 1965.

RIFKIND, CAROLE. *A Field Guide to American Architecture*. New York: New American Library (Plume), 1980.

STARLING, MARION WILSON. *The Slave Narrative*. Boston: G. K. Hall, 1981.

TROWBRIDGE, J. T. *The American Negro: His History and Literature*. New York: Arno Press.

———. *The South: A Tour of Its Battlefields and Ruined Cities*. New York: Arno Press, 1969.

WALKER, PETER F. *Vicksburg: A People at War, 1860–1865*. Chapel Hill: University of North Carolina Press, 1960.

WIKRAMANAYAKE, MARINA. *A World in Shadow*. Columbia: University of South Carolina Press, 1973.

"A Woman's Diary of the Siege of Vicksburg." *The Century Illustrated Monthly Magazine*, vol. 8 (May–October 1885). [Excerpts published anonymously. Later attributed to Dora Miller.]

PATRICIA CLAPP

was born in Boston and attended Columbia University School of Journalism. Her first novel, *Constance: A Story of Early Plymouth,* was a runner-up for the 1969 National Book Award for Children's Literature. Her other books include *I'm Deborah Sampson, King of the Dollhouse, Dr. Elizabeth,* and *Jane-Emily.* She describes herself as primarily "a theatre person"; she has worked with her community theatre for over forty years and still writes and directs plays for children. The grandmother of ten and great-grandmother of one, Ms. Clapp lives in Upper Montclair, New Jersey.

Ms. Clapp's most recent historical novel, *Witches' Children,* was based on the Salem witchcraft trials. ALA *Booklist* called it "a fine fictionalized account of a strange and disturbing episode," and *Bulletin of the Center for Children's Books* recommended it, praising its "vivid and convincing narrative." *Witches' Children* was selected as an ALA Best Book for Young Adults.